PICK YAR POISON

A KATIE MURPHY COZY MYSTERY

SUZANNE BOLDEN

LAUGHING DEER PRESS

CONTENTS

CHAPTER ONE

The Friday night chatter and music from the pub downstairs drifted up to those of us in the Waterford room. We were all getting itchy to get out of here, but Eve Brooks, our Pirate Festival chairwoman and famous local author, would have none of it. She was determined to finish our final committee meeting before the big event tomorrow.

Winnie's complaint about the wasted time in meetings like this was immediately silenced by Peg. "Let's just power through and finish this. I have a client meeting at my real estate office tonight. While you all are enjoying drinks downstairs, I'll be preparing an offer for a young family's first home." She clenched her jaw. "And I bet they'll bring their children with them."

"Well, cry me a Swanee River," Winnie said with a huff.

"Thanks, Peg." Eve looked down at her checklist before continuing, "I've decided we need to assign someone to handle Mayor Tim tomorrow. He's a sweet guy but easily distracted."

Tim Douglas was Seaside Cove's new mayor, voted in after the tragic death of Marvin Trimble. My Uncle Paddy dealt with him during the renovations of Paddy's Pub and called him a decent bloke. I was in Los Angeles at the time, taking care of my own matters. I only found out about his not-so-great appearance at the St. Patrick's Day event later on.

"Goodness gracious, he really made a mess of that Irish dance troupe's performance! Goofus trying to high step right alongside 'em," Winnie said. "Bless his heart."

A few snickers were suppressed, but I couldn't determine if they were triggered by memories of our mayor's awkward attempts at Irish dancing or due to Winnie's use of the classic Southern saying.

"Exactly my point. Do you want to take him on, Winnie?" Eve asked, tapping her pencil.

"No, ma'am. I don't have that kind of patience. Not at all," she said.

"I spoke to him when my third-grade class went to the municipal center for a field trip," Alan said. "When he found out I was on the committee, he pinned me down to let me know how eager and excited he was to perform those traditional Pirate Festival duties. His pirate costume is all set."

"Good lord, he's supposed to be portraying the mayor of the town that the pirates capture before they take it over. The guy shouldn't be wearing a pirate costume!" Winnie let out an exasperated sigh.

A pained expression crossed Alan's face. "I gave it my best shot, but I don't think he caught on to my hints."

"Precisely why we need a handler for him. He can wear his pirate get-up after the capturing ceremony." Eve didn't ask Alan to be the mayor's handler but simply told him he would be in that position. "I put you in charge of Tim."

"Put him in some pilgrim-looking outfit," Winnie added.

"Pilgrims didn't live here when the pirates came," Alan shot back.

"Well then, think of something to cover up his dang pirate outfit long enough to be captured," Winnie replied.

"She's right," Eve said impatiently. "The kids will be confused by pirates capturing pirates. Be firm with him, and don't forget he's got to have that giant key for Damien to take away."

"Yes, ma'am. I'll do my best."

Eve sighed. "Now, Katie, is Damien Falcon all set to conquer Seaside Cove at the end of the boat parade?"

"He's good to go," I said, glad to move along with our agenda. "His gorgeous boat, the *Black Pearl*, or yacht, I guess you'd call it, sailed into town on Wednesday. I took time to meet him then. He's quite a charming character."

"Handsome in a bad boy sort of way, isn't he? I'm looking forward to meeting him," she said with a wink. "He might provide inspiration for the bad guy in a book I have on the drawing board."

Peaches rubbed her hands and jiggled her shoulders suggestively. "I wished you'd assigned that task to me instead of Katie."

Eve just grinned and shook her head before turning her attention to our group's treasurer. "Fred, is there anything more you need for the bookkeeping you're in charge of?"

Fred Green stood and quickly said, "Nope. And may I be excused?" He held up his cell phone. "My brother texted that he's going to come up here and carry me out if I don't get downstairs pronto. He got into town today and is waiting downstairs with a new lady friend he wants me to meet. We're going to have dinner together with Fran."

"Alright, already," Eve said. "Meeting adjourned."

Peg and Fred bolted from the room while Eve collected her notes, and Winnie pushed herself up from her chair. "Glad it's still light out. I have a final rehearsal with the Galavanting Grannies. They cooked up a crazy routine for the parade. Hope these old legs can keep up."

That dance troupe was one part of the parade I'd be sorry to miss because I would be on the Paddy's Pub float, throwing out goodies for the spectators along the parade route. I hoped someone would capture a video of the Galavanting Grannies for me to watch later.

Participating in this committee was incredibly satisfying. It seemed ages ago since Mayor Marvin Trimble's murder in January. It happened before I left Seaside Cove to return to LA to sell my condo and my party planning business. Now I was happily back here with my Aunt Maeve and Uncle Paddy as part owner of Paddy's Pub. It was hard to believe how much my life had changed in such a short amount of time.

In just a matter of months, we'd held over a dozen parties and events here at the pub. From a fundraiser for the hospital to a Kentucky Derby party just last month. Paddy and Maeve were excited about the future possibilities for our venue. And so was I!

With June came the annual rush of tourists eager to take part in Seaside Cove's Pirate Festival. This would be a great opportunity for Paddy's Pub to shine. I went all out with decorations inspired by the famous Pirates of the Caribbean ride at Disney World for the large upper windows of our banquet area. Mel, our trusty male mannequin who greeted guests at the front door of the pub, was dressed in full pirate gear. He bore a striking resemblance to Johnny Depp's movie character, Captain Jack Sparrow.

As I closed up the Waterford room, I couldn't resist taking a moment to look at the view from the second-story windows. From here I could see all of Main Street below, and beyond that, the Wimico Bay and the Gulf of Mexico. The bay was already busy with boat traffic arriving for the pirate boat parade.

"Katie, will you be joining us downstairs?" Alan called back to me as he and Peaches left the room.

"You bet. I'll be right down."

CHAPTER TWO

The pub had been transformed into a pirate haven, complete with wooden barrels and Jolly Roger flags. The air was filled with the sound of lively sea shanties and laughter. Everyone on our staff got into the spirit of the weekend, wearing eye patches, bandanas, tri-corner hats, and white shirts with billowing sleeves or corsets and ruffled skirts. Lanterns with fake flickering candles adorned the tabletops.

"Hey guys, do you have your boat decorated for tomorrow's parade?" I asked as I joined my friends, Jack and Sophia Daniels. Happily, they'd moved their boat, Sophia's Delight, to our marina and were in the market for a Seaside Cove cottage as a second home. I'd met Sophia back when I visited another uncle of mine in Harmony, Wisconsin. She'd grown up there and returned to visit her brother. It was great to reconnect with her and Jack because they lived just a couple of hours away in Tallahassee.

"Yep, we've really gone all in. Jack has aspirations to win the parade so he can claim local bragging rights," Sophia said, smiling up at Jack.

"Aye, you wicked wench. You'll be swept up by my wild and dangerous allure!"

Sophia rolled her eyes in my direction. "He's been this way all day. I'm afraid to see what tomorrow will bring out in him."

Jack began belting out 'Yo ho ho, a pirate's life for me,' but was interrupted by an elbow to his ribs from his wife.

"What can I get you, my fair lass?" Our head bartender's outfit included a fake sword and pistol in his waistband, high leather boots and even skull and cross-bones rings. Liam's getup most definitely evoked the sense of adventure and rebellion of the pirate life.

"Good job with the outfit, Liam," I said, tossing him a thumbs up. "I've been looking forward to the rum drink you created for this weekend. I heard that the samples you gave out to staff were to die for."

"Aye, wise choice, matey!" Liam exclaimed with a grin. "An Emerald Buccaneer coming right up."

As we chatted, Jack leaned in and asked me about

tomorrow's boat parade. "Are you still planning on riding with us?"

I couldn't help but feel a twinge of envy as I remembered my duties for tomorrow's event. "Unfortunately, I won't be able to join you guys. I have to make sure everything goes smoothly with the *Black Pearl*'s takeover at Seaside Cove. Gotta keep the crew battle-ready!"

"That is one fine sailing vessel. I noticed her home flag is in the Cayman Islands," Jack said. "Must be nice!"

"But what's that about a battle?" Sophia asked.

"Ah, so you haven't heard about that part of the Pirate Festival. It opens with the decorated boats sailing around the cove. Then, the wild carousing pirates on the *Black Pearl* come back to the marina and claim Seaside Cove as their own. They will kidnap our brave mayor, Tim Douglas, and flaunt their captive in the land parade."

"Too funny!" Sophia said. "So, you're in charge of that?"

"Yep. When I went to meet up with Damien Falcon yesterday, we both agreed it was best if I sailed in on his ship. Probably a good idea, too. By being right there when the *Black Pearl*'s crew lands, I can whip up excitement in the crowd gathered in the marina. I've been told they get pretty rowdy by heckling the pirates when they come ashore," I said.

"You got a tour onboard the *Black Pearl*? What does she look like?" Jack asked.

"I'm embarrassed to say my mouth might have been hanging open for the entire tour," I said. "The whole thing felt so luxurious. Sleek, dark wood paneling and flooring. Plush white leather sofas scattered throughout the main living area. Crystal glassware lined up by the top-shelf liquor."

"Swoon-worthy? Is that what you were trying to say?" Sophia asked.

"Ah, yes. Most definitely," I said. "And the artwork. Original, I'm sure. And things that looked like artifacts. Clay pots. Even a wall of weapons. No plastic fake swords in there, but there were a couple of very real-looking ones. I could live on it year-round and be perfectly fine."

"Oh, lucky you! I've heard the owner cuts quite the striking figure. Like one of those bodice-ripping male models on the front of romance novels," Sophia said. "Watch yourself, Katie. Don't be sailing off to ports unknown to us."

"Tantalizing as sailing off sounds, no worries. He's too old for me," I quickly dismissed her suggestion, even though I wouldn't deny it had crossed my mind. "But it will be fun to pretend to be Grace O'Malley, Irish pirate queen, for the day."

"The Irish had pirates? Wow, I didn't know that. With your auburn hair, you'll be perfect," Sophia said.

"We'll miss you, but I understand duty calls. At least we've got Maeve and Paddy sailing with us," Jack said. "This whole thing is going to be so much fun."

"Here you go. Enjoy." Liam set down the exotic-looking drink and quickly dashed off to attend to a customer at the far end of the polished wood bar.

Out of the corner of my eye, I caught Fred Green waving. The man next to him must have been his brother, but the two couldn't have looked different.

Whereas Fred Green was short and slender with an impish air about him, his brother was tall, broad-shouldered, and carried extra pounds in his round belly. Fred tended toward a quiet shyness in crowds, but Bernie exuded self-confidence and ease, throwing back his head with laughter.

Fred was in his typical buttoned-down appearance, while his brother was casual in khaki shorts, a white polo shirt with aviator sunglasses hanging from the placket, and a captain's hat pushed back at an easy angle. Despite their different appearances and styles, both wore the same jovial, welcoming smile.

Fred came scurrying across the room with his twinkling eyes and a toothy grin. "Katie, can you please come and meet my brother? He loves this pub! I want him to meet the owner. Well, one of the owners, anyway. I tell you, he's very impressed."

I excused myself, telling Jack and Sophia that I'd see them in the morning.

"Meet my friend, Katie Murphy. One of the proud owners of this pub." Fred swept his hand toward the cozy establishment surrounding us. "And Katie, this is my brother, the one and only Bernard Green." Fred bowed and gestured toward his sibling with a flourish. A playful twinkle danced in his eyes as he did so.

"Call me Bernie, young lady," Bernard said. He reached to shake my hand, his plump, sturdy one encasing mine. "A pleasure to meet you. And this is my dear neighbor and special friend, Barbara. She's agreed to travel with me up to my old stomping grounds here in Seaside Cove."

Barbara's smile was warm and inviting. Her figure was soft and rounded, with gentle curves that were almost hidden by her colorful ensemble of a bright floral, hip-length top and billowing skirt that swayed with every step. Layers of costume jewelry adorned her wrists and neck, adding a playful touch to her outfit. Her hair was styled in loose curls, framing her rosy cheeks and sparkling eyes.

Bernie continued speaking, "I understand you're new here, Katie. Did Fred tell you any good stories about the shenanigans we got into when we were kiddos? Especially embarrassing for the somber undertaker father we had."

"He hasn't," I said, winking at Fred. "Regardless of those young rascals you may have been, I understand you both ended up in the family business."

"That's what Pop hoped for, and darn if it didn't happen," Bernie said. "I took over the family's small plant just north of here where we manufacture caskets. Steady business, one might say. As the owner of a casket company, I always found it ironic that my passion for sailing meant I might be buried at sea instead of in one of my own creations." His hearty belly laugh burst out again.

"Isn't he just so fun?" Fred looked admirably at his brother. "He really grew the business. Couldn't be prouder of him. He's stepped back from day-to-day operations, so he's not around here much anymore. I miss my big brother."

Barbara gently touched Fred's arm. "I'm good at reading people. We've just met, but I know that you are just the kindest and most compassionate man. You must be such a comfort to mourners."

Fred blushed.

"Isn't she an amazing person? So sweet!" Bernie beamed. "But let's stop discussing death and sorrow.

Please, bartender, get a round of drinks for myself and my companions."

Bernie's jovial personality and infectious laugh had drawn a crowd of other boaters who'd gathered around, slapping him on the back in greeting. I stepped away, blowing a kiss toward Fred. His short stature meant he was disappearing from view in the group.

Later that night, I made my way along the winding River Road in my trusty little golf cart, with the wind tousling through my hair. The moon cast a soft glow on the still waters of the Wimico River. The faint hum of crickets filled the night air as I stepped inside my temporary home, a houseboat anchored on the river's shore. I couldn't help but smile at the thought of the weekend ahead.

CHAPTER THREE

I'd been looking forward for days to this morning because I could dress up in a costume again. I loved wearing costumes! My party planning business back in LA would occasionally host themed events, and I always made sure to dress up accordingly. I'd packed my twenties flapper dress, a killer Super Woman costume, and my Louis XIV baroque style dress from a movie-themed party in the moving pods along with my furniture. Why on earth I thought they'd come in handy in a small Florida Panhandle town was beside me. They were still waiting to be unpacked, along with my other belongings, when I found a more permanent place to call home.

My Grace O'Malley pirate queen outfit had been

hanging on the door for a week now. I'd ordered it from a costume company in Los Angeles, knowing this festival would be the perfect place to play dress up again. After styling my thick hair into a disheveled look and adding some grunge-inspired makeup, I looked at myself in the mirror and was satisfied with the end result.

With an arrogant toss of my head, I said, "The world is yours, pirate queen…now, on with the show!"

My houseboat was docked upriver, north of the commercial fishing docks. Luckily, a bend in the river blocked my view of all the seafood being unloaded and afforded me a more pleasing vision of the far east shore of the river. But as I made my way to the marina, I saw I wasn't the only pirate on these early morning streets.

There were dozens of us in colorful outfits, with vests or frock coats over shirts tied with a sash. Many wore bandanas or pirate hats. Some even had fake parrots perched on their shoulders. A woman dressed in a long-skirted dress, wearing a dreadlocks wig and jingling beaded jewelry on her wrists, walked by holding the hand of a toddler proudly sporting his own hat and foam sword. Boisterous arghs filled the air as the day pirates tried to mimic the fierce, rugged bravado of the movie pirates they'd seen.

Liam had texted me that all things were a go for the

Paddy's Pub parade float. He was with Slim, the pub's head chef, at the municipal center parking lot, making final preparations. The staff would be dressed as pirates, of course, and we would all be throwing out colorful beads, eye patches, fake swords, and gold foil-wrapped doubloon candy to the children lining the parade route. The land parade route came to the marina, where the mayor would be captured by the pirates arriving by sea, then proceeded along the edge of the cove and up toward the downtown area.

Main Street itself had been closed to traffic, so festival goers could play the games, visit event vendors, and enjoy the food trucks without worrying about traffic. Skull and crossbones flags had been fluttering from the lampposts all week, and every store had outdone themselves with creative window displays, adding to the whimsical ambiance of the event.

The weather forecast for today was iffy. A storm was building on the Gulf waters, but last night's forecast had the storm turning more eastward and weakening in the process. All accounts had it making landfall closer to Cedar Key than to our shoreline.

"Ahoy there, mighty pirate queen. How dare you look so booty-ful?" Bernie Green called out as I walked past his boat.

"Ye be too kind, sir." I curtsied before pulling out my

hidden dagger and thrusting it in Bernie's direction. "But I fear ye offer sweet words to lure foolish souls into service on yer ship."

Bernie raised his hands high in the air and gave his hips a silly wiggle. "No, ma'am. I do not. Be off with you then if you doubt my good intentions."

"Aye," I said as I sheathed my dagger.

What a funny fellow he was. His love for the seafaring life was evident in the way his cabin cruiser meticulously gleamed in the morning sun. He had pulled out all the stops to win the best in the parade this year. Buccaneer flags, colorful streamers, skulls, and pirate paraphernalia adorned the boat. A blowup mermaid lounged on the deck. But it was the makeshift crow's nest perched on the upper enclosed helm that put it over the top.

Passing Sophia's Delight, I waved to Jack and Sophia. Paddy and Maeve were already onboard their boat. Everyone had dressed up in pirate gear and looked great. "Have fun, you all."

The *Black Pearl* was anchored at the far end of one of the docks because of its length. The rich, polished mahogany trim was a pleasing contrast to the richly layered black paint. The silver-trimmed port-hole windows and fittings glistened.

"I'm in awe," Damien said as he reached for my hand

to give me a lift aboard. "You make a most excellent pirate queen. You're portraying Grace O'Malley if I'm not wrong."

"I'm impressed with your knowledge of Irish pirates," I said. "And you, sir, look like a handsome, swashbuckling pirate from a Hollywood movie set."

He threw his head back with a low chuckle. "A pretend pirate on a movie set, my dear," he said before leaning in so close to me that the scent of his musk cologne enveloped me in its intoxicating aroma. I battled the urge to touch his tanned, powerful chest under the open-front white linen shirt he wore. "But I'd have to be a bit scruffier and smell like a monkey. And as you see, I enjoy my creature comforts too much for that," he continued with a playful smirk.

My breath caught in my throat. What had I gotten myself into?

"But perhaps that's what Grace O'Malley would like?" He ran his hand along his square jawline, almost caressing the short beard he wore. "Do you think I should get smudged up a bit? Would I look more dastardly that way? More the dirty pirate for you?"

Neither of us noticed the woman who emerged from the living quarters below until she spoke. "I can lend you my eye shadow."

I caught my breath. Damien gave me a suggestive wink before stepping back from me.

"Don't you think you've done quite enough with your appearance to play pirate for the day?" she said, adjusting the tight velvet corset she wore, giving her ample bosom even more exposure.

The heels on her black knee-high boots must have been at least four inches. How could she walk on a boat in those?

"Perhaps I have, Ariana. You look stunning. Especially sexy today. The pirates in this little town will be very impressed," Damien said before suggesting I enjoy the continental breakfast spread out on a topside table while we waited to leave the harbor.

I'd met this gorgeous South American beauty on Wednesday when I toured the ship. Damien had introduced her as a boat interior designer who was adding some new elements to his yacht. She might have been more than that from their interactions, but who was I to judge? He had an aura of command and power about him that I'm quite sure many women found attractive. Including me.

I served myself a steaming cup of freshly brewed coffee and selected a small croissant along with several pieces of the fresh fruit from the artistic arrangement on the platter. I could get used to this lifestyle. The pineapple juice's sweet tanginess tickled my taste buds. It must also have been dripping down my chin because Ariana tapped her finger lightly on her own chin. I quickly used my napkin to wipe off whatever had been there.

As the crew prepared for our cruise out to Wimico Bay, I remembered my Wednesday tour, where I learned that this sailing yacht slept ten, not including the crew's quarters. I could see where they were needed. This wasn't anything like pushing the engine's starter button on a small fishing boat and dropping the motor in the water to take off. But luckily, the crew moved with a rhythm familiar to them, and soon, our sails unfurled with a snap and billowed in the wind. We were underway on our pirate adventure.

Bernie Green was in his element as his captain navigated the *Cruising Along*. Bernie was grinning from ear to ear, waving and shouting greetings to the fellow boaters and spectators lining the shore.

As we sailed under the arched causeway, I saw more waiting boats out on the bay. I couldn't count them all. Some were there to watch the boat parade from the water, and some were decorated to be part of it.

We sailed past the shoreline, where children ran along, waving pirate flags, shouting and cheering us on. Damien, fully embracing his role, stood tall, his legs spread in a solid, commanding stance. He held a spyglass to one eye and a menacing sword in his other hand.

Occasionally, he'd brandish his sword in a threatening manner. That would always bring a responsive cheer from the kids, who'd wave their toy swords right back at him. I stood to one side of Damien, waving to the crowd gathered on the shore and thrusting my dagger in the air. The sea breeze loosened my auburn hair, and the building humidity puffed up my natural curls.

We turned to parade past Horseshoe Island, where more onlookers waited. The same excitement greeted us here as well. What an exhilarating journey!

As we began to make our way back to the marina, I took a moment to think about what it would be like to just tell the crew to whisk me away to a tropical island. I closed my eyes, feeling the salty air blowing across the bay from the Gulf of Mexico. I imagined myself going downstairs to change into a swimsuit and then lying on that huge chaise lounge on the deck. Staff would bring me a Mai Tai and some exotic fruit to nibble. I'd take a nap and wake up when...

A sharp sting hit my cheek. Ouch! What was that? I saw Damien grinning at me.

"What were you dreaming, my pirate queen?"

"Did you just throw something at me?" I asked, embarrassed to have been caught off guard like that.

"Just a tiny little ice cube," Damien answered. "Are you enjoying yourself?"

"I was," I answered. If only he knew he was part of the daydream I'd been having.

"Where were you sailing off to? We'll be battling the good villagers soon."

Oh-oh! I'd lost track of time. We would soon be in the harbor area. "How'd you know that's what I was imagining?"

"Just a good guess by the look on your face. We have a reservation to go through the Panama Canal in a few days." His voice lowered to an intimate tone. "Perhaps you'd like to join us?"

He'd read my mind. How'd he know what I'd been dreaming?

"That sounds like a crazy wonderful idea, Damien, but right now, this pirate queen has to use the bathroom before I help you battle the waiting hordes for domination of Seaside Cove."

I made my way to one of the bathrooms inside the yacht. I passed the displays of armament and other treasures but then realized I must have gone the wrong way because I ended up in the kitchen where I ran into Ariana.

She clicked her long fingernails on the crystal champagne flute in her hand. "Bathroom?"

I nodded.

She downed the remaining bubbly liquid from the glass. "It's back where you came from. Take a left at the jade mermaid in the niche."

I made it back on deck in time to proudly claim my role on the conquering pirate ship. Ahead, I saw the marina and Mayor Tim Douglas waiting to be captured. Luckily, Alan had convinced him to change his outfit for this part of the day. He wore a white untucked shirt over black trousers. Hooray Alan!

"Ahoy there, *Black Pearl*. Ye are not welcome in Seaside Cove. Be off with you and your evil thievery," Tim shouted as loud as he could. Alan nudged him, and he repeated himself in a louder tone.

The gathered townspeople played their role. They jostled and encouraged each other to boo and jeer, saying those scalawags and scurvy dogs won't take our town. There were even a few off with their heads thrown in.

Damien's commanding voice bellowed. "All hands on deck." His steely eyes scanned the scene of the determined crowd standing ready to defend their town.

Damien turned to me and, in a rough voice, said, "Grace O'Malley, tis this the place you wish to conquer?"

What? This wasn't in the plan. But all eyes, from Damien's to Alan and Tim's and all those gathered, turned to me. What to do? But then I scolded myself. You love role-playing. Have at it!

"Aye, Captain Falcon. Tis the very place I looked to plunder." I yanked my dagger out and raised it over my head while trying to make my eyes project malice and cunning. I was the wicked, powerful Irish queen of the pirates.

"Then it shall be yours, my love," Damien declared in his booming voice. He signaled me to follow him down the plank and toward the mayor, who actually looked scared. This was fun!

The crowd opened up as we moved toward Tim. The arrest was made by wrapping a heavy rope around the mayor's waist with his hands bound at his side.

"All cheer for Grace O'Malley…your pirate queen." Damien removed his pirate hat and bowed from his waist. "Tis all yours."

The key to the city appeared from somewhere and was presented to Damien, who pumped it high in the air, causing the conquered crowd to yell, "Hip, hip, hooray!"

With the arrest made and the loose, heavy rope still binding Tim, Hannah stopped us to make sure she got photos for the newspaper before Damien paraded him over to the float that would carry them in the parade. Ariana had joined us, and that took most eyes off of me. I tried to slip away to get on the Paddy's Pub float, but not before Damien embraced me and shouted. "Let the wild pirate rumpus commence!"

CHAPTER FOUR

With the parade over, it was Main Street's time to shine. It had become a sea of activity. I heard the splash of water and shouts of laughter coming from the Walk the Plank for Progress dunk tank, where all the money taken in would be added to the Parks Department improvement fund. Participants paid for the chance to throw a ball at the trigger target, hoping to hit it hard enough to see the mayor or one of our council members drop into the water.

At another booth, participants eagerly paid a small fee to guess the number of gold candy coins in a jar, with the closest guess getting all the candy. Two women were doing free face painting in front of the gift shop. Most of the young boys chose fierce looking pirate designs, while the girls often picked a mermaid style.

Winnie caught up with me on the street outside Paddy's Pub, where I watched Aunt Maeve manage the line of children eager to take a photo with Jolly Polly, the pet parrot brought in for the day.

My mannequin, Mel, AKA Captain Jack Sparrow, had one arm raised, showing off the hook hand that Slim helped me create. And thanks to some adjustments we made, he now had a peg leg as well. Luckily, I'd anticipated that Mel would become a draw for selfies and group photos and made sure the Paddy's Pub name was prominent from most any camera angle.

"Now ain't that there pirate statue clever? What a hoot!" Winnie burst out laughing, all the while twisting her neck up to fan herself. "Phe-wee, but it's hotter than blue blazes out here. The Galavanting Grannies dang near did me in. I'm fixin' to go inside the pub and get me some of that air conditioning."

"A good idea. Go in and cool off. The humidity is crazy today. My hair is already a big mess," I said.

"Plus, I'll tell you that tarot card reader gives me the heebie-jeebies. You know they call her the Witch of the Wimico round these parts?" Winnie's eyes darted nervously toward the modest tent pitched nearby. A hand-painted sign read MYSTIC MOON $5 tarot card readings today by the renowned Ms. Ella.

"Come on, Winnie," I said. "People just like to have fun with it."

But Winnie's angst was not to be denied. "No. No. No. Don't matter to me. I trust my guts on this one. Just look at those people, thinking she can tell 'em the future. Crystal balls? Bah. Not for me."

"I don't think tarot card reading involves predicting the future," Maeve said, trying to calm Winnie.

"Look, you can believe what you want. Me, I'm getting myself a cold sweet tea and taking a load off." Winnie stomped on into the cool interior of the pub.

"Do you know the tarot card reader?" I asked Maeve.

"I don't know her personally, but I didn't want Winnie's ranting to get out of hand. Oh no, hang on, Katie!" Maeve dashed off to protect Jolly Polly from one of her more aggressive young admirers. "No pulling the parrot's tail feathers!"

Down the street, a large wooden box, looking like a raised flower bed, was filled with sand. There Tyler Berman, owner of the Rum Runner restaurant on Horseshoe Island, was helping three young kids dig for buried pirate treasure. A woman with the same blonde hair as Tyler cheered them on. Since Maeve appeared to have things under control here, I decided to walk over and say hi.

Tyler greeted me. "I missed the conquering pirates'

scene, but I heard you and the guy from the *Black Pearl* really kicked it up a notch."

"Thanks. It was fun. Are those your nieces and nephews visiting from Wisconsin?"

"Yep. I told them about the pirate festival, and they decided to come down a little early this year to enjoy it."

"Looks like they love being with their uncle. Why don't you bring them over and get a photo with Jolly Polly when you find your treasure here?" I said.

"Sounds good," he said. 'Haven't seen you out on the island lately."

"I need to get over there and enjoy one of your beach sunsets."

He grinned playfully at me, reminding me of the first time he had ever introduced me to oysters at a beach-side restaurant. "Well, if you do, I'll treat you to some fresh oysters," he teased, making my heart flutter just like it did that night.

Remembering the night he'd first taught me how to eat that delicacy, I said, "It's a deal. Say, we're having a band play later, during the fireworks. Will you be around for that?"

"I have to get back to the Rum Runner for our Saturday night crowd. But I will keep an eye out for the fireworks going off between me and you."

It took me a pitter-patter heartbeat to get the gist of

what he'd said and realize he meant the fireworks in the bay between the island and Seaside Cove. "I'll be watching them, too."

My mission now was to find a snow cone and cool myself off. But I was distracted by a jolly voice shouting out, "Grace O'Malley...you gorgeous thing!"

Bernie Green slid in next to me with a big grin. "Love this festival. Those Blimey Beignets keep calling me back for just one more. And the Shiver Me Timbers Tacos...wowza, they sure lived up to their name."

He rubbed his tummy before removing his pirate hat and wiping the sweat from his brow with the back of his hand. "No spice like that for Barbara. You met her last night, right?"

"I did. A lovely lady."

"Care to join me in the pub while Barbara gets her cards read? I'm not even sure what that means, but she was excited when she saw the tarot tent. Me, not so much. No hocus-pocus for this guy."

"I'd like to be a fly on the wall and see what a tarot card reading looks like," I said. "I've never done one, but it's sort of intriguing, don't you think?"

"I'm pretty much a what you see is what you get kinda guy. Now Barbara is more into fairies and mystical things. Oh, have you seen my brother Fred around? I owe him a pint for putting up with me."

Bernie fanned himself with his hat to fend off the stifling heat and humidity. "Oh, here's Fred now. Would you let Barbara know we're inside?" And he was off to greet his brother by slinging an arm around his shoulder and leading the way into the cool interior of the pub.

Bernie didn't give me a chance to respond, but I did pass the request on to Maeve before continuing my snow cone hunt. Across the street, at the Sew-Sew shop, Marge had set up a craft table for the children and her son Jesse was helping with it.

Marge looked so much like her son with her thick, dark brown hair. She told me how much she appreciated me jumping right in and volunteering for the festival committee. Then, as she smoothly slipped another glue stick into a little pirate's hand, she asked, "Are you worried about the storm changing course yet again and making for a rough night on the houseboat?"

"I hadn't thought of that, but I was told it's in a protected spot, so it shouldn't be anything like the open water on the Gulf," I said.

"I can always check in on you," Jesse offered in a teasing tone. "You know I'm not really very far from you via the River Road."

"I think I'll be okay," I said, even though his offer was tempting. "But Marge, I had a question for you. Do you know anything about Ms. Ella, the tarot card reader?"

"Besides her being called the Witch of the Wimico? Better to ask my son. Jesse is sweet with Ella," Marge said, smiling up at her son. "He even buys eggs from her chickens for his restaurant. And he helps with her groceries and such. The poor woman has such a sad story. In fact, it was Jesse who brought her into town today and helped set up that tent for her."

Jesse shrugged modestly. "No biggie, I'm glad she agreed to come. Ella likes her solitary life in the forest and some people are uncomfortable with that, I guess. And it's not just eggs that I get from her. She is an expert on finding the best mushrooms. My cook makes the yummiest cream of mushroom soup with them," Jesse said. "Why do you ask?"

"Just curious. Will I see you two at the dance later?" I asked.

"Sure will," Marge said. "I don't want to miss the fireworks."

"I'm planning on it," Jesse said. "Save a dance for me, Katie?"

* * *

Our community park was nestled between the Wimico Bay shoreline and a small hill where the grand old mansions, including Eve Brooks home, stood. River

Road followed the edge of the bay and passed by the fishing pier. Tonight people sat either on the rough boards of the pier dangling their legs above the water or on the wooden benches that edged the pier, more to be a part of the festivities than to do any fishing.

The cover band had been playing in the park gazebo for over an hour. They played music familiar across the generations of people gathered here. I noticed lots of families had spread blankets on the grassy slope to people watch, listen to the band, and station themselves for a good view of the fireworks that would be shot off from the barge anchored in the bay. Out on the cove, boats bobbed gently in the approaching twilight.

Marge was seated with Maeve at one of the picnic tables. I went over to ask her if Jesse was coming.

"He had a problem back at the River Lodge that he needed to attend to. Both Maeve and I have been abandoned by our dancing partners," Marge said.

"She's right. Paddy stayed back at the pub to help the bartenders. But I'm okay with sitting these songs out. Not many from my era of music anyway," Maeve said.

Of all the people I didn't expect to see, here was Damien Falcon. He came walking right toward me, carrying two plastic cups. And no Ariana in sight. He smiled and nodded toward me, handing the plastic cups to Maeve and Marge.

"Here you go, ladies. Now, can I have that dance you promised me?"

My mind raced. I didn't promise him a dance. What did he mean? But I realized my mistake when he reached for Marge's hand, and they walked to the dance floor.

"Isn't he just the nicest, mean-looking guy?" Maeve asked.

"Mean-looking? I think he's handsome," I said.

"Maybe that's the wrong word for what I'm trying to describe," Maeve said. "At first, I thought he had a hard edge to him. But actually, he turned out to be quite pleasant. Marge and I were sitting here at this picnic table when he came up and offered to buy us a soda to wet our whistles. Next thing you know, quiet Marge Shaw just up and asked him to dance with her. You never know. You just never know." Maeve chuckled.

And with that, the first boom of fireworks sounded, and the night sky lit up, all eyes shifting to watch the display, oohs and aahs echoing across the hill.

CHAPTER FIVE

Sunday morning, I took my golf cart into town and decided to cruise through the marina area before heading over to Paddy's Pub to help with brunch.

Yesterday's Pirate Festival had gone off with barely a hitch, except the digging for pirate treasure game ran out of prizes, and one inebriated pirate tripped and heave ho'd himself right into the water, only to be rescued by someone on the fishing pier.

The day's highlight was probably the children's costume contest because, after years of tears, some very smart planning allowed for more age groups and categories to get prizes this time around. The evening in the park was perfect, even though I didn't get much dancing in. Damien left after dancing with Marge, saying he had to meet someone back on the *Black Pearl*. I'll admit I was disappointed neither Jesse nor Tyler could make it, but my cousin Liam got me out on the dance floor for a few numbers.

Jack was wiping down the rear seats on his boat when I pulled up at the edge of his pier.

"Ahoy matey," I called out. "Hope you two had fun yesterday. Sorry I didn't get to see more of you."

"Hey Katie, how's it going? Want a cup of coffee with us?" Jack asked.

"I'd love to, but I'm heading over to the pub to lend a hand for brunch. Say hi to Sophia for me. How long are you guys staying in town?"

"We're taking off later this afternoon. Back to the office for me," he answered. "But the brunch idea sounds good. Maybe we'll see you there."

The *Black Pearl* glistened in the morning sun. Damien and Ariana were seated on the deck with another couple I didn't recognize. What a life!

All was quiet on the *Cruising Along*. Bernie and Barbara must be sleeping in.

I pulled into the pub's back parking lot and entered through the rear door, where typical kitchen noises filled the back hall. I poked my head in to say good morning to Slim, our head chef, before walking toward the front of the building. There I found Uncle Paddy directing customers to have a coffee on him in the Coffee Corner while they waited for a table.

"Ah, lass, glad to see ya. Can you lend a hand as the hostess here? We've had a lot of the tourists in town showing up for brunch, thanks to that extra promotion you did. It worked like a charm!"

"A great place like this is easy to promote," I said before shooing Paddy back into the pub. I'd posted a few social media items featuring photographs of our mouth-watering food and our welcoming atmosphere. It seemed to do the trick. Plus, pirate Mel and all the photographs taken with him drew a fair share of new eyes to Paddy's Pub.

Eve Brooks, along with her son Greg and daughter-in-law Hannah, were seated near the hostess stand. I congratulated Eve on the success of all her hard work leading the committee this year.

"Count yourselves lucky that storm passed by," Greg said.

"Agreed. The day was near perfect. Not much of a breeze to blow all that humidity away, but at least no rain," Hannah said. "I got some terrific shots for the newspaper. They'll be great to increase promotion for next year's event. But that mayor being captured scene… wow, Katie! The best one yet."

"I'll see you later at the wrap-up meeting," I told Eve before I left to seat some new guests.

Fred Green came bouncing over from the snug where he and his wife were seated. "Katie, looks like you're in charge here. I wanted to let you know that Fran and I are in that little hidden place. The one back in the corner. We're waiting for Bernie and Barbara. I've tried calling him, but he doesn't answer. Probably walking over and didn't bother to pick up."

"I just was in the harbor and saw the *Cruising Along*. Pretty quiet there," I said.

"Ah, those lazy bums! Haha. Bet they're out cold. A day like they had would exhaust anyone. I saw them swing-dancing well into the night. Don't know how long they stayed out there after Fran and I left," Fred said. He fussed a bit, peering out the front doors, turning his head right and left as if willing them to appear.

Who did show up at that moment was Seaside's chief of police, Darnell Jensen, with what looked like most of his staff. "Morning Katie. Looks like the place is hopping. I called ahead, and Paddy said he'd save a table for us. I want to treat my guys and gals to brunch for the long hours they put in yesterday."

"Go right on in then, Darnell, it's set up to your right." Even in my short time here, I recognized many of them as they moved along to their table. Blaire, Hannah's niece, stopped to say hello at the Brooks table, and one of the other officers hugged an elderly woman enjoying brunch with her friend. A benefit of living in a small town was that familiar faces made everyone feel connected.

Fred caught me as I walked back to the hostess stand. "Katie, it's just a short walk to Bernie's boat. Okay if Fran holds down the booth here? I know you all are super busy, but I'm going to kick Bernie's lazy butt out of bed."

"No problem, Fred," I said. "You go on ahead. Take the back door. It's just beyond the kitchen. It puts you right out on River Road."

It took a second for Fred to understand. "Ah, got it. Much thanks. I'll hurry back."

Within minutes, I noticed Darnell talking to Fran Green. Then he grabbed one of his fellow officers and came to me. "Katie, can you do me a favor? An ambulance has been called for Bernie on his boat. I'm heading over there now. I just let Fran know that Fred isn't coming back here. He wants her to come to the marina. Would you help and bring her down there?"

"You got it, Chief."

After a quick explanation to Paddy, I went to Fran.

She was gathering up her reading glasses, cell phone, and purse. She was shaken up. "Is Bernie okay? Why didn't Fred call me?"

"I'm curious too, Fran. Let's go there together. My golf cart is in back."

CHAPTER SIX

The wailing sirens of an ambulance faded into the distance as Fran and I hurried to the marina. We found Fred seated on a metal bench at the spot near where his brother's boat was docked. His usually bright, sparkly eyes were dead-looking. As soon as he saw Fran, the tears started flowing. She sat next to him and enveloped the small man in her arms, soothing him with the sounds you would offer a crying baby.

"He's gone," Fred finally spoke, his words breaking with a sad sob.

What? That big, robust man? He was so full of life. What had happened? Damien stood nearby with Ariana and the couple I'd seen on his boat this morning. They might know more about this awful situation.

"It's suspected that there were dangerous levels of carbon monoxide in the boat's cabin," Damien explained in a dry matter-of-fact manner. "It seems like a major oversight on the part of the boat owner caused his death."

"Bernie was usually so careful with that sort of thing." The woman shook her head from side to side, her eyes wide and filled with a mixture of confusion and disbelief.

"Katie, meet Victoria and Richard Ingalls," Damien said. "Victoria is Bernie's ex-wife. We assisted Fred after we heard his wail coming from the boat. Another boat owner here is a doctor, and he's the one who diagnosed the cause of Bernie's death. Carbon monoxide poisoning. Not a bad way to go. You just don't wake up."

Ouch. That was rather harsh sounding. True, I suppose, but cold at a moment like this. "But how did the doctor come to that conclusion so quickly? I heard that the gas is odorless?"

Damien shrugged. "You'd have to ask him. I'm going for a walk to Gator's Seafood Market. Anyone want to join me and help me pick out some fresh seafood for my dinner?"

"I will," Ariana said, taking his arm.

Richard peered over the top of his white-framed

sunglasses to say, "Nice to have met you, Katie." Then, shoving his hands in the pockets of his white shorts, he too turned to head in the direction of the seafood market a couple of blocks south.

Victoria stayed, her face shielded by a floppy-brimmed hat.

"I'm so sorry, Victoria. Bernie seemed like a nice man."

She took off the hat and let out a heavy sigh before looking up at me. Her eyes showed hints of sadness but also a sense of calm and clarity. "Thank you. He was a very nice man. Our divorce was awkward and unpleasant, but it was a long time ago. I'd better go over and sit with Fred for a minute. This is a big hit for him. He always looked up to his big brother. Excuse me."

With their siren off, another ambulance pulled up, and the EMT staff boarded the boat with a stretcher.

Skull and crossbow flags fluttered and snapped in the morning breeze. A seagull landed on the pretend crow's nest and began squawking. The salty sea breeze mingled with the scent of diesel fuel from the boats. With Victoria on one side and Fran on the other, Fred stood as his brother's body was removed from the boat he'd loved.

Darnell and his officer followed the stretcher off the

boat. Their eyes squinted against the harsh glare of the sun. Darnell quickly donned his sunglasses before joining Fred and Fran to stand at attention beside them as the ambulance drove away.

CHAPTER SEVEN

I offered to take Fred and his wife back up to the pub's parking lot to pick up their car, but Fred gave me a sad smile and began to walk slowly away. Alone. As though he didn't hear me.

"Thank you, Katie, but we're good to walk back. Might kind of help us get our bearings," Fran said. "We'll be going right up to the hospital to see how Barbara is. The doctor thought her survival might have been because she was wearing a CPAP mask for her sleep apnea. Plus, she was sleeping in the forward bedroom, not with Bernie in the bigger quarters. We never really knew how close their relationship was. If you know what I mean."

Fran's whisper of the last words didn't surprise me. Her generation would not have asked if Bernie and

Barbara were more than friends. But not sleeping together might be a clue, until Fran added, "Course Bernie had that god-awful snore."

Or that!

I watched Fran catch up with Fred and take his hand.

Victoria choked back a laugh. "She's right about that being a possible reason they weren't staying in the same room. I remember that gravelly rumble! And it might have been a vanity thing for her, too. I imagine wearing one of those night-breathing masks can't be very sexy."

"You told Damien your ex was usually so careful. What did you mean? Careful about what?" I asked.

"Bernie loved his toys. Like his ATV, his motorcycle, his jet ski, and especially his boats. Always kept them in top-notch shape. He had a very good understanding of mechanical things and was always very careful to do timely maintenance. If his boat motor or generator were acting up, he would have had them fixed. And he certainly would have kept his CO detectors operational. Safety was a big thing for him. For all his jolly, flamboyant behavior in public, he was actually quite an organized man. He craved it, in fact. That's what made him such a successful businessman."

Her words were barely audible as she muttered something else to herself. I leaned in closer and asked, "I'm sorry, I didn't catch that last part."

She shook her head and replied, "Never mind. Please excuse my rambling." After clearing her throat, she continued, "It appears the police are restricting access to the boat. Do you think they suspect it may not have been an accident?"

Darnell's officer hung a no trespassing sign on the piling next to *Cruising Along* and was securing the boat's entrance gate with a padlock.

"Hopefully it's just a temporary measure. Chief Darnell is careful and cautious. He doesn't jump to conclusions." Even though they'd divorced years ago, Victoria had once loved Bernie and I sensed she was trying to distance herself from those mixed emotions.

"I don't think I've met your police chief because Richard and I rarely get back to the area. I wasn't surprised to see Bernie here, though. At the heart of it, he was still a small-town kid. I'm glad to see he'd gotten over the midlife crisis he suffered. There were several decades younger girls around for a few years. Barbara didn't strike me as a gold digger, but she could have been fooling everyone. Well, enough of my blabbering. I'm going to see if Richard has gotten some fresh seafood for us."

Now that was an info dump! Our chief had an open-door policy. He instilled in his staff the knowledge that hard as they might try and good as they might be at their jobs, they should never underestimate the power of the public. He encouraged them to let him know if they needed help and to admit if they'd been wrong about something. Maybe Victoria should talk to him. But she was hurrying off toward the seafood market.

"Sad thing. Bernie seemed like such a nice guy," I said as I joined Darnell.

He leaned against the back of a bench and finished the note he was making and tucked the pad back in his pants pocket. "He was a favorite around here. Local kid made good and all of that."

"So, it was carbon monoxide poisoning?"

"Yep. It'll be confirmed at the morgue, but it's pretty safe to say that's what did him in. When Fred first discovered his brother's body, he thought it was a heart attack. But when he found Barbara out of it in the other bedroom, he was confused. Plus, I'm sure that confusion was amplified because of the heavy concentration of carbon monoxide still in the air Fred was breathing."

I sat down on the bench and Darnell joined me. "How'd you figure out that's what caused it? Damien said a doctor might have helped you."

"Right. He was here in the marina on one of the other boats. He came aboard and pointed out the cherry-red coloration of Bernie's skin surface. It's a classic symptom of the poisoning. It appears that Bernie was running the boat's air conditioner off his gas generator. I know the harbor master put out a warning about the possibility of electricity outages for the boats because of the excess load on the shore power over the weekend."

"The heat and humidity were hitting Bernie hard yesterday," I said.

Darnell nodded and removed his sunglasses to wipe the sweat from his eyes. "Same weather today it looks like. But the death would have been prevented if the CO detectors had been functioning correctly. We have yet to figure out why the batteries in his carbon monoxide detectors had been disabled. But it's a clue that this might have been more than a tragic accident."

I leaned forward at hearing that. "Do you think someone did it intentionally? Victoria, Bernie's ex, just said something like that herself. She said Bernie was careful with things on his boat. It surprised her that he let that happen."

"I don't know yet. But I'd like to talk with Fred later. He was groggy and befuddled when I got here and practically fainted, so I sent him outside to get fresh air. And now he's gone."

A man in mechanic's overalls approached us, nervously twisting his hat with his hands.

"Josh, just the man I wanted to speak to," Darnell

said. "Katie, this is Josh Thomas, our local go-to mechanic for boats. He might be young but has a terrific reputation here."

Josh nodded politely. "What happened to Mr. Green?"

"Carbon monoxide poisoning. I'd like you to take a look at his generator if you would. We are…"

Josh's mouth fell open in shock as he heard those words.

Darnell paused and looked at Josh. "Josh? What is it?"

"I worked on that generator just this past Friday, sir. The day they arrived. They were having trouble with it. I disabled the detectors while I was working on the generator because otherwise, they would have kept going off, even with windows and doors open."

Darnell perked up. Josh had his complete attention now. "Well now, Josh, that's interesting. You reconnected them when you were done. Right?"

"Of course I did. I'd never leave something like that unfinished. In fact, I called the boat captain that evening to explain what had been wrong with the generator. He thanked me and said he was grateful because he himself was leaving town for a few days after Saturday's boat parade and that the boat would remain in the harbor, so the owner would appreciate having the AC running high."

Darnell's brow furrowed as he asked, "Did he happen to mention the batteries in the detectors? Were they reconnected?"

Josh's face paled and he stammered, "Um...I don't remember if we discussed it. But I know I reconnected them. I'm positive!"

"Calm down, Josh," Darnell reassured him. "No one is accusing you of anything. You have a great reputation around here. There must be some other explanation."

Josh's eyes darted frantically, a look of panic and confusion etched on his face. The memory of Friday must be replaying over and over in his mind. Had he reconnected the batteries? The weight of potential consequences if he hadn't would loom over him like a dark cloud.

CHAPTER EIGHT

Back at Paddy's Pub, the Sunday brunch rush was finished, and I took the chance to explain to Maeve and Paddy what happened to Fred's brother.

"What a bleedin' shame. So tragic it is. Who'd be daft to mess with the detectors?" Paddy said.

I debated whether to share Darnell's conversation with Josh. It seemed unfair to Josh and might harm his reputation. It could lead to more unnecessary rumors flying around as they do so easily in small towns. My internal debate was cut short when Jack and Sophia joined us.

They'd heard the basics of what had occurred. "I noticed the local boat mechanic at Bernie's craft late on Friday," Jack said. "I haven't needed the guy for anything yet, but he seems to have a good reputation among the other boaters. But that day I heard raised voices by Bernie's boat. It got pretty heated. I assumed it was the mechanic, but not sure who the other guy was. Could have been the captain or even Bernie, I guess."

"That mechanic is Josh Thomas," I said. "I was there when Darnell talked to him this morning. He did work on the boat and admitted he disconnected the detectors so they wouldn't kick on while he was working."

Jack nodded. "That makes sense. Those detectors are so sensitive nowadays. Poor kid. Hope he remembered to hook them back up. Otherwise, he's in a boatload of trouble. Paddy, would you mention what I overheard to Darnell when your coffee group gets together? It could mean something or nothing at all."

"Will do, Jack."

"Speaking of the captain," I said. "Josh said he left town after the boat parade. He probably doesn't even know what's happened."

"Ah, good point, Katie," Paddy said. "And with Barbara in the hospital, he might not have been notified yet. Hopefully, she'll know how to reach him."

"Not a good ending to the festival weekend. Have you heard how Barbara is doing? I couldn't believe she survived," Jack said.

"I don't know, but Fred and Fran were heading over

to the hospital to check on her," I said. "I'm sure Darnell will be talking to her as soon as she's able."

Sophia and Jack said their goodbyes, telling us to reach out to them if we needed anything.

* * *

Later on Sunday, the festival committee gathered in the Waterford room to close up the books and go over things. What went right? What went wrong or could have been done better? Eve also wanted everyone's input to help compile a report to give to next year's committee. But she was having difficulty keeping the members focused. Everyone was talking about the sudden and unexpected death. The word murder even began popping up.

"Is it true that the batteries in the CO detectors were taken out?" Peaches asked. "Unbelievable that someone would want to murder Fred's brother. Where is he, by the way?"

"I certainly didn't expect Fred to attend this meeting," Eve said. "He has to deal with his brother's death and is probably helping the woman Bernie was here with. I understand she's still hospitalized. Katie has offered to take the money from the split-the-pot raffle and the Pirate's Loot resale over to Fred tomorrow," Eve said. "Now, can we please complete the report from each of you? Peg, what did you hear from the vendors? Is there anything specific they liked, and were there any complaints or concerns?"

Peg stood and opened her spiral notebook. "The walk-the-plank dunk tank was a big hit and should most definitely return next year. The owner did suggest...."

"Maybe he oughta steer away from dunkin' anyone wearing a phony beard and a wig. Did y'all see when that fancy councilman, all decked out like some swash-buckling pirate, ended up chasin' and divin' for his parts and pieces when he was dunked?" Winnie chortled loudly. "Lordy, but I wish I had a camera on that one."

"Right. I saw that, too. Felt kind of bad for the guy." Peg continued with her brief rundown on the vendors, including the fact that the tarot card reader was very satisfied with her audience but wouldn't commit to next year.

"She's an odd duck," Winnie said. "A recluse. I know she had trouble back in the day, but geez, you'd think she'd gotten over it by now. Who got her to come in for the festival?"

"I think Marge's son talked her into it," Alan said. "You could ask Fred. Someone had to have paid her vendor fee."

"What's her story?" I asked. Jesse had given his

account of Ella and I wondered how much more there must be to her story. Surely someone here could fill in more details. But Eve was already on to the next committee question.

"Peaches, who received the most votes from the boat parade?" Eve asked.

"I had to toss a bunch of voting slips out because they wrote in the *Black Pearl*," Peaches said. "And we all know you are not allowed to vote for this year's conquering pirate ship. Though my goodness, my heart went pitter-patter when I saw you being Damien's pirate queen, Katie. And with all those swarthy pirates from his crew lining the boat's edge. I almost ran up and said take me!"

Alan laughed. "My wife said the same thing. Cheers to Katie for that moment. And to our intrepid mayor for playing his part to a tee. But now, back to announcing the winner and our conquering pirates next year."

"The winner was number twenty-three! Let me see." Peaches referred to the list of boats that had registered to be part of the parade, running her finger down the list. "The winner is *Cruising Along*. I'll contact the owner..." She peered closer. "Bernard Green."

Winnie snorted and spit out the words, "For god's sake, girl. That's the dead man."

Peaches, her reading glasses slipping down her nose

in shock, looked up at Winnie with wide eyes. Her usually calm demeanor faltered as she stammered, "Oh my. We've never had anything like this happen. What should I do?"

"Look, it's easy. Who came in second?" Peg's words seemed to help Peaches regain her composure.

"Ah…I'll have to recount…I guess," Peaches stuttered out her reply. "Give me a minute."

"Right," Eve murmured in a patient tone. "Now, Katie, for your report on the dance and the fireworks. It looked like that all went very smoothly."

My report briefly summarized the positive feedback the band and the fireworks received. I also mentioned that I had asked the band if they were available for next year and said I would be sure to have someone contact them. They appreciated if that could be done soon, as the summer months were their busiest. Additionally, I noted that the fireworks group was disbanding at the end of this year, so it would be crucial to book a new one as soon as possible.

"Okay, thanks, Katie. And thank you, everyone, for all your great work on this committee. I think that's everything for now. If you'll all get me a typed page or two of your duties and information, I'll compile them in a folder to hand off to the next chairperson."

"How about a round of applause for our chair-woman?" I said. "She did a wonderful job."

As everyone stood and prepared to leave, Eve asked if I could give her a ride home, saying she'd walked over but had something she wanted to ask me about.

On the drive to her house, Eve explained that her next book was a drug smuggling thriller set on the Florida coast and the Key Islands. "It was spooky how this tragedy happened because it relates to my current research. I wanted to bounce an idea off you. It's been bothering me since I heard about Fred's brother this morning."

I pulled the golf cart to a stop in front of Eve's home, a large mansion perched on one of the highest points in Seaside Cove. Here, we had a sweeping view of the bay and across to Horseshoe Island.

"By all means. Go ahead," I said.

"I'm just into the rough draft now, but with the research Greg has already done, I'm shocked at how prevalent drugs are here and how very dangerous they've become."

"Hey, coming from LA, I know what you mean. It's a terrible scourge. But what was it you wanted to bounce off of me?" I asked.

"Do you have any sense there are illegal drugs involved in what happened to Bernard?"

That question sure set me back on my heels. I started going through the things I knew so far, and none of it contained a hint of drug use or drug smuggling. I shook my head. "I don't have any sense of that, Eve. Nothing that I heard or felt would have made me think about drugs being involved."

"Blaire said that the chief has requested the remaining boat owners stay here in Seaside Cove another day, if possible. What does that sound like to you?"

"I suppose just a cautionary step. Like he strung up crime scene tape earlier," I answered. "My first thought would be that he wants a chance to talk to them and ask if they'd seen anything unusual."

"Mine too, but she said he is also pulling available records of where the boats are registered."

"Hmm…that's intense," I said.

"There's something else, Katie. The Green family has an interesting history, along with a family secret they've tried to bury. I'm not the only one who knows about it, but there aren't many of us left," Eve said as she looked out toward the bay. "It came back to my mind while working on this book. The incident had been quite a scandal when it occurred. Fred's parents tried to quash it, and they did a pretty good job of it. I don't know if Darnell is aware of the story."

"Then go talk to him. He has an open-door policy. And if you are this concerned, it might mean something. Can't hurt."

"No, just my overactive author mind. It was way in the past," Eve said. "Sorry about cutting you off, but if you want to learn about Ella Winchester, I know her history. I'll tell you when we have some time."

It had been a restless night because I had Eve's conversation stuck in my head. She never did tell me the Green family secret, which left me curious as to what it might be. But back to the present. Would someone have wanted Bernie out of the way over drugs? Was the fun, gregarious man a drug smuggler himself? Or did he make a discovery that someone didn't want to come out? It seemed so farfetched. But our location on the Gulf of Mexico and the miles of uninhabited coastline did make the area tempting for smugglers.

I decided to call Jack to see if there were any active investigations involving drug trafficking currently happening in our area. Since he's an FBI agent in the Tallahassee Resident Agency, he might know something.

I gave him a quick call. He told me he'd see what he could find out.

When I got to Fred's house with the treasury paperwork and money, he seemed to be in a daze. His usual bouncy and vigorous movements were subdued. When I asked about Barbara's condition, he simply said that she was getting out of the hospital today without providing any further details.

However, when I told him his brother's boat won the award for the best-decorated boat in the parade, it brought a smile to his face.

"That would have made him so happy," Fred said. "He should be here to enjoy that and start making plans to lead the parade next year."

"I know I just met him, but I could tell he was something special. I'm so very sorry for your loss," I said. "Do you want to go over anything with the accounting on the festival? No rush at all. Just whenever you're ready."

Fred looked up, and the smile was gone. He was trembling.

"Fred, what is it?"

"Something's been heavy on my mind," Fred blurted out. "I just have this deep sense of foul play involving my brother's death. Maybe I'm still in shock? Oh, I don't know." He dropped his head into his hands. "I just can't sit here and do nothing. I just can't."

"Tell me what you're thinking, Fred. I'm here to listen."

Fred echoed Victoria's suspicions from yesterday. He explained that Bernie was meticulous about safety measures and would have made sure all detectors were working properly after the generator had been worked on. He felt someone must have tampered with the boat's detectors while Bernie and Barbara were at the dance.

"Do you know of anyone here who would have wanted him dead?" I asked.

"I don't. Not at all. This must sound crazy to you. But my brother still has connections here in the area. Did you know he and his partner own a casket manufacturing plant north of here? Oh yeah, you heard that Friday night. Sorry. Everything's so muddled up in my head. But maybe someone at the plant? A disgruntled employee? The business has changed. People request cremation more now. So maybe they are in financial trouble?"

"I'd heard about that too. Who was his partner?"

"His ex-wife Victoria. In their divorce, each kept half of the company. Over the years, it made them both a great deal of money. Or so it appeared. Bernie semi-retired to the Keys, and Victoria moved away from here as well."

"And now, if it's losing money, what are you suggesting, Fred? That she could have done this for some reason?"

Fred looked shocked and then shifted uncomfortably in his seat.

"You don't have to answer that. I'm sorry I put you on the spot," I said.

"I couldn't answer because I never even thought of that possibility, Katie. I didn't mean Victoria. Oh, I don't know what I meant. My family was in the funeral and burial business for generations. We're proud of what our family built. But there was a shameful and dark time as well."

Ah, so he's bringing up the family secret time that Eve mentioned last night, I thought. "And from that long ago time you think there is something lurking. Maybe even something to do with what happened? That it might be a motive for someone to hurt your brother?"

"Oh dear. I don't know if I should share this. It's such a stain on our family, but it's been weighing so heavily on my mind that I just need to get it off my chest. Fran knows about it, and she thinks I'm letting it grow into an oversized beast. Those are her words. She says that it's not that big of a deal. But I think it is, or rather was."

Fred began nervously pacing in the living room of their modest ranch home. On the walls hung dozens of family photographs. All the eyes seemed to be following the back-and-forth pacing of Fred. He was working himself into a tizzy and I was getting seasick myself. I wanted to shout stop walking like that, but Fran did it for me when she came through the front door and saw what was happening.

"Fred, stop that pacing at once! You're making yourself sick, and I'm sure Katie has better things to do than sit here watching you work yourself up into a lather."

"Hi, Fran." I shifted uncomfortably in my seat, suddenly feeling out of place. "Just stopped in to express my condolences and give Fred the treasurer's stuff from the festival."

Thanks, Katie." Fran gave me a grateful nod before turning her attention back to her husband. "I suppose Fred shared his family's story. The one that he's somehow connecting to his brother's death?"

"Well, he started to, but then…." I gestured toward Fred, who was still pacing.

"Oh, for god's sake Fred. You're making way too big of a deal about this." Fran turned to me, and a humorless laugh slipped out as she plopped down on the sofa. "Let me explain what my husband is fretting about. During the 1920s, the Greens, like many during that time, were not doing well financially. It was the Great Depression, after all. So, they had what I believe is now called a side hustle." "When I explain, you'll see why he can't stand to see that restaurant on the island called the Rum Runner."

I heard a whimper from Fred before Fran continued. "The Green men hid whisky in empty coffins they built at Woodville Casket Company. They got the booze from gangsters who smuggled it in from the Bahamas and Cuba. The caskets were shipped all over, and it was, I thought, quite a clever, albeit highly illegal, scheme. Eventually, other locals got involved in making bathtub gin and having stills out in the woods, and they also used the Green's unique system to transport it."

"Now, wait a minute. That was a hundred years ago. Caskets are still being made, right? They weren't put out of business. What is it you're worried about now?" I asked.

"You want to tell her, Fred?" Fran's hard stare at her husband didn't help him get his words out.

"Hmm...I don't even want to say this out loud. It's scary stuff. And I don't even...oh my...I'm so confused."

Fran let out an exasperated huff. "Oh, for heaven's sake. What has been on Fred's mind is that, with the current situation and financial stress on business, along with the memory of illegality and booze smuggling fresh on his mind, there is a possibility that pressure might have been on Bernie or someone in his circle, to..."

Was she going into ramble mode, too? It slowly dawned on me. My stomach churned at the thought. "Wait! I get it. Fred's worried Bernie was carrying on the family tradition. Only instead of alcohol, he was smuggling drugs?"

Fran's smile grew wider, confirming my suspicions without needing to say a word.

CHAPTER TEN

Through the pub's coffee shop window, I saw my Aunt Maeve engaged in conversation with Eve, who had her usual effortless, put-together look. Somehow, her outfit, a simple blouse and slim-fitting trousers, looked different on her than it would on me. Not a hair was out of place on her short, stylish do.

"Good morning, Katie," Maeve said as I joined them.

I gave Maeve a hug and then greeted Eve. "I'm glad you're here. I went to drop off the treasurer's things at Fred's, and one thing led to another. I ended up having a very interesting conversation with Fred and his wife."

"How is he doing?" Maeve asked as she brought me a coffee.

"Seems sort of lost. Like he's in a daze. I guess losing

your big brother under such odd circumstances will do that."

"Poor guy. He's got a lot on his plate now," Maeve said. She excused herself to assist a customer who was admiring one of the handcrafted, quilted wall hangings. Maeve had put forth great effort in promoting local arts and crafts, evident in the beautiful merchandise that filled this space. My eyes caught sight of the adorable shopping totes with Coffee Corner printed on them, a perfect souvenir to remember this charming little shop by.

"Eve, can I share what the Greens talked about? It has me kind of worried. You know them well. They've been in this town and in the same line of work, like forever."

She chuckled. "Sure, go ahead and share, but let me guess first. Fred brought up their big family secret that they circumvented the law during prohibition. Is that what he told you?"

"That's right. But now Fred has projected past misdeeds into present times. He is worried that someone in the family may be doing something illegal again."

"I guess it could be possible," Eve said with a grin. "My mystery thrillers have to have intriguing plot twists. And Fred's idea sounds like it could have potential. Let's think about this. Is Bernard Green, the jovial, rotund Floridian, an illegal substance smuggler as his ancestors were? Or is he merely an innocent bystander enjoying his life while, beneath the surface, his factory minions have created a path for illegal drugs to be dispersed throughout the United States, wreaking havoc and poisoning the nation's youth?"

I couldn't resist the temptation to join in. "And has the competition masterminded his death to cut out the middleman? Or did his devious, conniving business partner decide to do him in and keep all the ill-gotten gains?"

"Ooh, I know." Eve leaned in, twitching her eyebrows. "How about this? Had his murderer been threatened that he had to do it or else the whole operation would be revealed to the law! And then the murderer would be caught, too. But if he eliminated the big guy, all would be okay. Things would stay as they were."

"Threatened by who, though?" I asked. "And who is the murderer? The factory minions!"

"Because they were smarter than he gave them credit for, and they...rebelled!" Eve burst out laughing. "Just like in those Despicable Me cartoons!"

"What are you two laughing about over here?" Maeve asked.

"You're missing all the fun. Take a break and join us for a second." Eve pulled up another chair for Maeve.

"Well, maybe for just a second," Maeve said.

"We were brainstorming possible scenarios for a murder," I said.

"How is that funny?" Maeve asked.

Eve and I just looked at each other and shrugged.

"Guess I had to be here?" Maeve suggested.

"Something like that," I said. "It was just nonsense. But maybe now Eve will tell me the story behind Ella Winchester, the tarot card reader. Did you know about tarot card reading growing up in Ireland, Maeve?"

"Ah, lass, we aren't some backward country, you have to remember. Certainly, we had those readers there as well. Not my cup o' tea, but I've seen it done."

"Why do the people whisper amongst themselves about her, and the kids call her a witch?" I asked.

Eve took a moment and a sip of her tea to collect her thoughts before beginning the story. "I understand she was not always the solitary figure she has become, residing deep in the forest, away from prying eyes. At one time, she had a family. A husband and two young children whom she cherished more than life itself. They had a happy and settled life as small farmers.

"But one fateful, awful night, a raging fire engulfed their home. All her possessions were destroyed, along with the loves of her simple life. Her children and husband. Ella barely escaped with her life. In the aftermath of the tragedy, consumed by grief and guilt, she made the decision to retreat into the heart of the forest, back to her original family home, which still stood. It had been abandoned, but the work to restore it brought strength to her weakened body, and the dense foliage there shielded her from the whispers of sympathy in the outside world."

"Sure, and it's no wonder you're an author, Eve. You have a way with words." Maeve took a deep breath. "The scars some folk carry. Poor woman."

We were all distracted by Barbara showing up at the Coffee Corner. I breathed a sigh of relief that she hadn't heard Eve and me making up stories about a murder. That would have been more than awkward.

"Barbara, so good to see you up on your feet," I said, standing to give her a hug. "We're all saddened by Bernie's passing and so sorry for your loss."

"Thank you," she said. "I was released just a little while ago. Fred took me to the boat to pick up my possessions. I'm not in any condition to travel yet, so I booked a room at the Fulton Inn. Could I have an iced sweet tea, please? I need a little pick me up."

"Of course," Maeve said. She motioned Barbara to take her chair and went to prepare her tea.

Barbara explained her plan to fly back home to Key West in a few days. "The tarot card reader's words to me on Saturday have been haunting me. Did I mishear her? I'm feeling so unsettled. And I must help find out what happened to my dear friend Bernie, too."

"Remember, tarot is not fortune telling," Eve said.

"I understand that," Barbara said. "But I'd like to speak to Ella again to help me understand some of what we talked about. I don't know how to find her, though. I was hoping someone could help me with that."

After hearing Eve's explanation of Ella Winchester's history, and now listening to Barbara wanting to find her, I decided to offer my help. Barbara thanked me profusely, and we exchanged phone numbers before I excused myself to take down the pirate decorations in our building.

It would be fascinating to get out into the woods and see how Ella lived. I could reach out to Jesse to see if he would give me directions to her house. Or better yet, have him show us the way. A plus because then I'd get to see him again, too.

Jesse didn't answer his phone, so I left a brief message explaining the situation. I hadn't met Ella and didn't know if he had a way to reach her so the visit wouldn't be an unwanted surprise. Maybe she didn't like to talk with people who she'd read for. I certainly didn't want to intrude on her privacy.

I hoped to talk to Barbara later when we went out to visit Ella's forest home. Ever since Victoria mentioned the possibility that Barbara might be deceiving everyone, I couldn't shake the thought from my mind. People have told me that I can be too trusting and naïve. Sometimes, evil can hide in plain sight, even within seemingly ordinary people. Could this be one of those cases?

The day flew by. Taking down the Pirate Festival decorations and carefully storing them for next year took up a good part of the day. I started on the Fourth of July decorations. I redressed Mel as an Uncle Sam and began hanging the red, white, and blue bunting when my cell rang.

It was Jesse returning my call. He apologized for taking so long, but he'd been out on the river guiding tourists. He was totally agreeable to showing us the way to Ella's house and felt she wouldn't mind if we dropped in. In a warm tone of voice, he added that it was good to hear from me and he looked forward to seeing me tomorrow.

CHAPTER ELEVEN

The next morning, Jesse met Barbara and me at the junction of River Road and the entrance to his fishing lodge. He was leaning against his ATV, looking outdoorsy handsome in his Shaw's River Lodge olive drab T-shirt and faded blue jeans. I introduced him to Barbara, explaining she was a dear friend of the man who had died.

"I heard about that." Taking his hat off and holding it against his chest, he said, "My deepest condolences, ma'am. Are you okay? I understand you were hospitalized yourself."

Barbara assured him she was feeling much better and effusively thanked him for helping us find the tarot card reader.

We followed his ATV as he headed north for what I

estimated to be about two miles. At the point where an old, rusted mailbox, leaning at a precarious angle, stood, he made a sharp left turn away from the river. The road narrowed and became only two-wheel tracks that the low-growing scrub brush and grasses threatened to bury. The forest, filled with cypresses, oaks, and magnolias, became denser. The tree limbs grew so long that they reached across the drive. We were in deep shadows now and the shade cooled my skin.

Ahead, I saw a small wooden bridge that had seen better days. Jesse didn't hesitate to drive over it, so I followed. A musty, earthy smell rose from the murky water of the tributary beneath us. How many branches of the Wimico River reached far into these swampy lowlands? I couldn't tell but imagined they were countless.

Jesse came to a halt. I had assumed we were on a driveway all along, ever since seeing the mailbox where we'd turned in, but I couldn't see a house. With the rumbling of the ATV motor off, an eerie silence enveloped us. It took a couple of seconds to hear the constant hum of swamp insects and the occasional bird call.

Jesse got out and said, "Pretty secluded, isn't it?"

"I'll say."

He helped Barbara out of the cart. "We head this way."

The footpath we entered took us under an arch that was hand-woven from sturdy vines. From the center of the arch hung a crescent moon sculpted out of wood. Tendrils of feathers, tied with thin string, fluttered beneath it. Dried flowers, nestled in bundles of live moss, were carefully tucked into little pockets throughout the arch.

We didn't walk far before we came to a small clearing. The gray, weathered home seemed almost a mirage in all the wildness we'd passed through. But it was real, and so was the sturdy little barn and outhouse behind it. Chickens roaming free threw out noisy squawks. A horse in a fenced enclosure looked up at our arrival but then nonchalantly went back to munching on the grass at his feet. The three goats with him quickly slipped under the fence rail to investigate us.

As we approached the home, the front screen door screeched open, and Ella stepped out on the low porch. The sun glinted off her hair, revealing strands of silvery gray woven in with the dark brown. I'd seen her briefly on Saturday, where she'd been wearing a caftan and a headscarf, but she was dressed very differently today. She wore a faded plaid shirt with rolled-up sleeves and well-worn, loose-fitting jeans. Her hair was pulled back from her weathered face, etched with fine lines.

"Ms. Ella, hope we didn't interrupt something important," Jesse said.

"It's always nice to see you, Jesse. And I see you've brought me company," she said, tipping her head in our direction. "Barbara, I remember you from Saturday. How nice to see you again! But I don't believe we've met, young lady."

"Ms. Ella, this is Katie Murphy. She lives in Seaside Cove and gave Barbara a ride out to see you."

"Hmm…that's nice. But why are you here, Barbara? You have a question for me, don't you?" Ella asked gently. "Please. Come sit on my porch."

"I can't stay, Ms. Ella," Jesse said. "But I brought you some fresh catfish. Caught just this morning. Katie should be able to find her way back to River Road on her own."

I tried to hide my disappointment that Jesse wouldn't be staying. "We'll be fine. I appreciate you bringing us here."

"Hope to see you again soon," Jesse said. "You take care, Ms. Ella, and I'll be back Thursday to get more eggs."

"Very nice man," Ella said. "Now, what did you want to ask me, Barbara?"

The first words out of Barbara's mouth were, "You look so different!"

With a low chuckle, Ella said, "For readings, like I did at the pirate event, I dress to fit what people expect a tarot card reader to look like. I consider myself a competent, proficient reader, but in the sort of setting like the festival, the customers want more of the crystal ball fortune teller look. So that's what I give them."

"But I took it totally seriously, and I thought you did as well," Barbara said in an accusatory tone.

There was the slightest hardening in Ella's gaze. "Most people ask for a reading on a whim. They see the tent and me in my getup and think of it as a game. Entertainment. Something fun to do on a lark. That is why I rarely involve myself in the type of setup I did on Saturday. But it does earn some income to pay for staples the land doesn't provide me."

"What you told me wasn't real?" Barbara scoffed. "And here it's been churning in my mind, and it was all bunk."

Well, this wasn't going well, I thought as I reached down to push away the goat nibbling at the edge of my shorts.

"That's not what I said, and I certainly didn't mean to imply it. Please, both of you, come and sit beside me while I explain."

Ella didn't take the one chair on her porch but instead lowered herself to the edge of the porch boards, with her feet resting on the ground. I sat next to her. Barbara, perhaps fearing it would be hard for her to get back up, stepped up to the porch deck and chose the chair.

"Do you remember the pattern of the card spread I did for you?"

Barbara nodded. "Yes. You called it a Celtic Cross and used ten cards."

"Part of my process is intuiting the beliefs and honesty of the person I'm reading. I sometimes use only three card spreads, but most often five. When you sat down, I immediately sensed you were different. Serious and open to an honest, forthright experience. Those readings bring me the most satisfaction."

Barbara nodded. "Thank you. I'm sorry if I snapped just now. But I felt very in tune with you and the cards the moment I looked into your eyes. That's why I wanted to see you again, in person. I have some questions. But first of all, the man I talked about has passed away."

Ella gasped. "You feared something bad happening to him, didn't you?"

"And I feel so wrong to have even thought that and said it out loud."

"It came out in our reading. The things we talked about brought it out. You shouldn't think that us speaking of it made it happen. Would you like to talk to me about him?"

Watching Barbara's physical reaction to the question, I sensed she was hesitant to talk in front of me.

She didn't speak. We sat silent. The horse snorted softly as a tabby cat slinked across his path.

Finally, I broke the silence. "May I stroll around your place? I see all the artwork you have on display here, and I'd like to get a closer look at it. I just love the way you use natural materials."

"Please do. Some people think I created the pieces to scare little children away. As though I have droves of children coming here." Her pleasant laugh relaxed both Barbara and me. "I know my being a recluse confuses and even frightens people. And yes, I know I'm spoken of as the Witch of the Wimico. But the pieces you see here, I do for me. They bring me pleasure and help me remain grounded in Mother Nature. Thank you for taking note of them."

As I roamed the paddock and the edges of the forest, admiring the random artwork, I began to notice a few unusual pieces, almost tableaus, things mixed in with the natural elements. A small child's toy soldier rested in the embrace of a bird's nest in the fork of a tree branch.

A huge mushroom extending out from the large split in a tree trunk shaded a green glass marble carefully supported by peeled-back bark. Were these her children's things salvaged from the fire?

Wandering behind the house, a few spoken words carried to me as though floating on the breeze. Page of wands. Sevens of swords. Opposing energy. Pentacle. The empress. Reversed.

Moving further away to give them privacy, I spent a few more relaxing minutes in this oasis of calm before I heard Barbara calling my name.

Ella took hold of Barbara's hands as they said good-bye. By their expressions, it appeared she got the answers she came for.

Then Ella spoke to me, "Thank you for bringing Barbara to me. We had a revealing and honest conversation."

Barbara opened up to me on the way back to Seaside Cove. She thanked me profusely for bringing her here to see Ella. With a sense of embarrassment, she explained that she had asked for a romantic love life reading from Ella. She shared that her feelings for Bernie had been growing, saying that they were great companions, but she would have loved more of a romantic relationship.

"I thought he was thinking the same thing, but lately, I've been overhearing him taking calls from Victoria. I was getting jealous, and I don't like feeling that way. This trip was going to be special. He wanted me to meet his family, then she showed up here, too! When I saw the Mystic Moon sign, I just had to give it a shot. I felt the reading went well, and Bernie and I had a fun evening dancing and watching fireworks. I put any of the doubtful thoughts I had out of my mind. Then, bam! My sweet Bernie died. I felt so lost. How could this be? Was there something I missed in the reading? But Ella helped me understand all of those feelings and helped me put things into perspective. She should be a psychologist!"

After getting that off her chest, Barbara was quiet and pensive for the rest of the drive back to the Fulton Inn. She seemed to wake from a dream when she realized where we were and asked, "Katie, could you please take me to the police station instead? I received a call from the chief of police yesterday that he would like to talk to me. I believe I'm ready to do that now."

"Sure, I'd be happy to. I'll wait for you here. It's been a long day, and you just got out of the hospital."

"That might be best if it's not too much bother. I'm

still a bit weak, and even that short walk at Ella's house tired me out."

Blaire, Hannah's niece, was behind the front desk today. After walking Barbara back to Darnell's office, Blaire was excited to tell me that a group of friends were coming down to Paddy's Friday night for a bachelorette party. "I hope you'll be around. I'd love to have my friends meet you."

"I helped with making arrangements for that party! I'm so glad to hear you're part of it." I'd been so busy since I moved here that I hadn't found a group of friends closer to my age yet. Blaire seemed like someone who'd be fun to hang around with. I would make sure to be at the pub on Friday night.

CHAPTER TWELVE

When I poked my head into Paddy's office Wednesday morning, I saw Chief Darnell was with him. "Oops! Sorry to interrupt. I'll come back later. Just had a couple of questions about the bachelorette party booked for Friday night."

Paddy waved me in. "Katie, come join us."

"I was just bending your uncle's ear," Darnell said. "Since he was the Chief of Police in Harmony, he is my go-to guy to bounce police matters off of. And Katie, in my humble opinion, it seems you share that family trait of clear-headedness."

Did he really think that? Hmm...kind of flattering. He must be remembering my help with the issues affecting his investigation into Mayor Trimble's death. Lots of tangled threads there.

"That's why I begged her to be a part of my crazy dream of opening an Irish pub in Florida. You saved the day girlie. Without you this pub might have withered away." Paddy motioned for me to sit down next to Darnell.

"Let's just say it was beneficial for both of us," I said, taking my seat and wondering what all this was about.

"Aye, Katie, you've a good head on your shoulders, like Darnell pointed out. He was just running through the suspects in the case of Bernard Green's death."

"Or lack thereof," Darnell said. "I heard it was you who brought Barbara to my office yesterday, Katie. That was nice of you. She mentioned that the two of you visited with Ella Winchester."

"We did. I was happy to take her out to the woman's house. On Monday, after her release from the hospital, she got a room at the Fulton Inn and then came here to our Coffee Corner to get a tea. She said she'd delayed her plans of booking a flight back to Key West. She felt she could do something to help law enforcement find out who wanted to kill Bernie."

"Did she ever think she might have been a target, too?" Paddy asked.

I leaned forward. "I'm not sure about that. But she said something about that tarot reading concerned her, and she thought talking to the reader would help clarify things."

"Can you embellish on what she said after talking to Ella?" Darnell asked.

Not wanting to repeat all the deeply personal things Barbara had confided in me, I fumbled around for a few seconds with how much I should say before Darnell spoke. "Listen, Katie. I appreciate that you and she had a private conversation. I'm not looking to embarrass the woman, but I want to compare notes about what she told me."

For the next few minutes, Darnell and I broke down what Barbara had said to each of us. What she had told him was almost exactly, word for word, what she and I discussed. Her growing romantic feelings for Bernie. Her feelings of jealousy over noting him talking more to his ex-wife. And then the upsetting feelings she had when she saw Victoria was also here in Seaside Cove for the weekend. Afterward we both agreed that Barbara thought that there might have been a rekindled romance between Bernie and his ex-wife.

"I'd like to add something suggested to me. Perhaps Barbara should be checked out. Like maybe she was a gold-digger. Not the typical one. She wasn't a curvy, gorgeous young woman, but maybe in a more sinister way?"

Darnell quickly dismissed the idea. "She's not a criminal in the disguise of an overweight, past her prime woman, if that's what your person suggested. She's financially very well off herself. You might not know it to look at her. She doesn't flaunt it. Would this someone want you to be distracted? Like, look at that over there instead of me?"

"Good point," I said.

"Was it Victoria Ingalls?"

I nodded.

"Now she's someone who would have a motive...or so I thought until Fred told me more about the Woodville Casket Company," Darnell said with a sigh. "He explained that he was his brother Bernie's main heir. But instead of getting half of the company, he would receive the benefits of a life insurance policy, as per a partnership agreement drawn up when Victoria and Bernie divorced. As it played out, she now owns the entire company."

"So, this Victoria is your prime suspect?" Paddy asked.

Shaking his head, Darnell continued, "Still a suspect, but not the prime one. After talking with Barbara yesterday, I got a clearer picture of the situation. Because of the tarot reading on Saturday, Barbara had a very candid conversation with Bernie. He reassured her that all the phone conversations between him and Victoria were not romantic but rather were about business."

"Then waking up Sunday morning, what a shock! Poor Barbara, being hospitalized and out of it for over a day and then suddenly learning all that happened," I said. 'So now, since Victoria will own the place and she doesn't need Bernie's approval to sell it, would that have been her motive?"

"That's why she's still a suspect on my end. Did Victoria just speed up the process of selling out by getting total control?" Darnell rubbed his chin. "There's that one other thing that Fred and Barbara both told me. Bernie had recently learned that the plant was in serious financial trouble. Fewer coffins selling because of more people going for cremation. Increased cost of supplies and shipping. Bernie was staying in town primarily to dig deeper into the situation at Woodville and had made plans to visit there on Monday."

"I've been thinking about the captain of the *Cruising Along*. Did Barbara tell you anything about him?" Paddy asked. "After all, he could easily have undone the batteries himself before he left on Saturday."

"This journey from Key West to here was the first time she met him because she'd been on a Mexican vacation for the prior two weeks. She explained that Bernie's previous captain was a younger man and now had a family, so he decided he wanted to travel less. I called the Key West harbormaster, asking if he could give me the name of the new captain. He asked around and got his name."

"Good detective work," Paddy said. "Will the captain be back soon?"

"I sure hope so, but I can't compel him to. I've spoken to him on the phone, and he denies he tampered with the batteries. He, of course, mentioned the issue with the compressor and needing it to be completely operational, what with the possibility of power outages from a storm and overloaded circuits in the marina. Josh's repair of the compressor was discussed and his thoughts about that. But I still want to bring him in for questioning. Always good to look someone in the eye. He doesn't appear to have a motive. But a couple of things showed up on a deep dive background check that concerns me. No illegalities, but some oddities."

"Okay, so you have Victoria, the captain, and maybe Josh as suspects?" I asked.

"Yes, Josh Thomas is one. There's that report of overhearing an argument regarding his work on Bernie's boat," Darnell said. "Throw in Barbara, too. There are some common threads I'm following. But Katie, I'm glad you're here because I wanted to ask you something specific. Did you get a look inside the *Black Pearl*? Damien's going to be leaving town, and I really have nothing to hold him, but his name has come to my attention. First time was from Josh. I questioned his crew, and they said yes, they used Josh for a little item they didn't have a part for. They seemed rather close-mouthed, but I suppose the rich don't like their staff talking about goings-on aboard."

"Yes, I was onboard a couple of times. It was my job to make sure the owner of the winning boat from last year understood their duty to perform this year. So, I met up with Damien on Wednesday. Then, of course, on Saturday for the parade."

"And did you see anything unusual?"

"Not really. But Sunday morning, on my way to help out at the pub, I decided to take a ride through the marina. Damien was having coffee aboard the *Black Pearl* with Victoria and husband Richard, along with Ariana, who he calls his boat's interior designer, wink wink. But then later, when all the attention was on Fred, I remember sensing how detached Damien seemed. He left with the other two to get some fresh seafood at the fish market while Victoria stayed behind and talked to me. That's when she put the bug in my ear about Barbara."

"So that Damien fella is still in town?" Paddy asked. "I'm sort of surprised about that. After a quick assessment of the man and his style, I would have thought he'd blow this small town before I could count to ten."

"He's a man of many personas," I said. "He noticed Marge Shaw and Maeve sitting on the sideline at the dance and bought them a soda. Then he had a dance with Marge."

"Ah, Maeve didn't tell me that!" Paddy said. "I'll be darn. That Marge is a pretty woman."

"But not like Ariana," Darnell said.

"Chief, I'm a little shocked. Please tell me you noticed her only in a professional capacity." I didn't give him time to answer, but I heard his soft chuckle. "The point being he was kind and gracious to us small-town folk. As to anything that caught my attention on his yacht…" I shrugged.

"Did you sense he knew Victoria and Richard prior to arriving here in Seaside Cove?" Paddy asked.

"Great question," Darnell said. "I would have thought not, but the fact Damien was here last year for the festival and won it would mean the odds are high that they met then. Victoria loved coming back home to

Seaside Cove. So maybe asking Victoria's opinions of the man might be worth discreetly checking out."

"You said Josh brought him up to you," Paddy said. "Has he done anything else to make you suspect him?"

Darnell's eyes darted uneasily toward the windows, looking out to the marina before continuing. "He balked at my request that the boaters remain until I've had a chance to question them all. Damien told me that unless I was going to charge him, he assumed he was free to go. With an arrogant attitude, he assured me he was not dropping off the face of the earth but had an appointment to enter and travel through the Panama Canal. He even mocked me by questioning if I knew where that was. Like I'm a small-town cop, and he's such a worldly man who did not want to miss the window of time he'd been given to travel to the other ocean."

"Wow...rude bugger," Paddy said. "What do you make of it?"

"Not much," Darnell said with a shrug as he stood and put his hat on. "He's entitled to move on with his life. Oh, and Katie, thanks for having Jack reach out to me. I had no idea he was with the FBI. Nice to have a direct line if I should ever need it."

"You're welcome."

"And I owe you a thanks, Darnell," Paddy said. "I hired that accountant you suggested. She's a bright woman and will be a good fit for our small business. I learned she handles other restaurants in the area."

"Great to hear. Now I'd better get going. I've got a couple of dogs waiting for me." Darnell lifted his nose and made an exaggerated sniffing sound.

"Ah, those sorts of dogs," Paddy said. "For the boat?"

Darnell adjusted his hat and winked at us. "Yep. Drug dogs find the smallest traces."

CHAPTER THIRTEEN

Peg picked me up at the pub, excited to show me the three houses she had scheduled for us to look at today. This process had been put off long enough. My six-month houseboat rental was almost up, and I needed to find a permanent place to live. If push came to shove, I knew I could stay with Maeve and Paddy again, but I really looked forward to getting a place of my own and finally unpacking my possessions sitting in containers shipped from Los Angeles.

I had romanticized living in a houseboat. One like the Tom Hanks character lived on in that old movie *Sleepless in Seattle*. But cute as my current abode was, it was not at all like his houseboat, and this was not Seattle. Now I wavered between just finding a nice rental, which would be easiest, and I'd have no issues with upkeep or repairs, or bite the bullet and buy something. At this point, I was open to either one. But buying meant a bigger financial commitment and any house would have to be goosebumps generating for me to even consider it.

My top priority was to have a water view. From my LA condo on the thirty-second floor, I could catch a teeny tiny sliver of the Pacific Ocean if I stretched out to peek around the corner of my balcony. Here, I wanted to go all in and be able to look toward the Gulf of Mexico and catch both sunrise and sunset colors on the water.

"Hop on in," Peg said as she pulled up in front of Paddy's Pub. A custom decal on the side of her sleek white golf cart displayed her real estate office logo and contact information. Built-in pockets displayed brochures, and cup holders held chilled bottles of water.

"Wow, you are too much! This cart is crazy cool, Peg."

"Why, thank you, Katie. I like to get my clients pumped up about this house-hunting journey they are undertaking. Speaking of undertaking, how's Fred doing? You've seen him since our final committee meeting, right?"

"He's getting along okay, I'd say."

"I've heard this was all over drug smuggling stuff, but I don't believe all that gossip. What about you?"

"Seriously, drug smuggling?" I kept my answer noncommittal even though I knew Darnell was taking drug-sniffing dogs to go over Bernie's boat. How were those dogs doing? What would it mean if they hit on a scent? I would suppose Darnell's drug dogs will be noticed in the marina, and everyone will hear about it soon enough.

Peg handed me a house flier to look at as she pulled away from the curb, heading toward the first house we'd be seeing. "I still wonder if it wasn't all just a terrible mistake. That happens. People make mistakes."

She had a good point. No matter what both Barbara and Victoria said about Bernie, he could have missed the disconnected CO detectors. But that would mean that Josh forgot to reconnect them.

"All three houses we're looking at have water views, per your request. This first one is a small seaside stilt cottage on Horseshoe Island. It is at the top of your price range, but it might be perfect."

"Wow, really? That's great! I think I'd rather be here in town, but I'm open to looking."

We raced along in the golf cart lane that took us over

the causeway to the island. The sparkling water below energized me. It felt good to get out in the fresh air after this morning's discussion with Paddy and Darnell.

The beach house's setting was amazing! Every direction offered stunning water views. The gentle rustle of seagrass and the rhythmic lull of waves against the shore created a calm feeling, and the random calls of seagulls seemed to welcome me. What would it feel like to walk up these steps to my own house on the beach every day? I leaned on the upper balcony railing to breathe in the crisp air with its hints of salt and seaweed. But the mood was broken as soon as I stepped inside. This place needed work. A lot of work. No goosebumps here!

"By your expression I can see we didn't reach perfect on this one. How about we grab a quick lunch here, as our next appointment is not for another hour? I love the beach seating at the Rum Runner. Okay with you?"

"You don't have to ask twice," I said.

We'd settled in after placing our order. A seafood salad for me and crab cakes for Peg. "I must admit, I wished I had your job on the pirate committee. To sail on that beautiful yacht, the *Black Pearl*, would have been wonderful."

"It was something, that's for sure. The interior was so amazing. But way more boat than one man needs."

"If you can afford a crew to sail it…" She shrugged and took a bite. "I say go for it. Kind of like if I could afford a housekeeper, I'd get a bigger home. And maybe a second home here on the island. Or, like Bernie Green, a place in Key West. The Green family has apparently done well dealing with death. Yech, I wouldn't want to be in that business, but I guess someone has to do it."

"Guess so," I said as I watched Tyler approach our table. Maybe a dumpy beach house here might be worth it if it included seeing more of him.

"Nice to see you ladies enjoying the sunshine. I'd like to offer my congratulations on a successful Pirate Festival. Or, in the words of my niece and nephews, can we live here with you, Uncle Tyler, and be pirates?"

"Super cute. I'm glad they had a good time," I said.

"I'm on a mission to get Katie Murphy into a more permanent place," Peg said. "We just toured a home here and now are going to check out a couple back in Seaside. Might you want to extoll the positives of living on the island?"

Tyler spread his arms out, sweeping across the Gulf waters in front of us. "This!" Then he leaned on the table, getting much closer and throwing in a bonus. "Plus, I'd offer you free use of my jet skis anytime you want to go out. Though that offer has been made before now, and you have yet to take advantage of it."

"I'm so sorry, Tyler. You're right. How about next week? Remember, I've never done it, so could I get a ride-along with you the first time?"

He gave me a reassuring smile before standing up from his chair. "Absolutely. Next week it is, and I'll hold you to it. Have a good day, and good luck with the house hunt." He stood up from the table and gently squeezed my shoulder before walking away.

* * *

Back on the mainland, our first stop was a cottage similar in size to Kenmare Cottage, Maeve and Paddy's home. It was located only three blocks from them, but its water view was minimal. On to the final one for the day.

One block back from the larger homes that looked out over the bay from their perch atop the hill, this one was a newer home done in a minimalistic style. A little too hard-edged for me. Still no goosebumps.

"May I suggest an apartment that my realty firm manages for the homeowner? I think it might be perfect for you. It's been updated but maintains the original woodwork and unique architectural details. I brought a key along just in case."

"Sure, Peg. I'd love to see it."

We hopped back into her golf cart and drove just around the corner to one of the mansions on the hill.

Goosebumps! Just looking at the outside of the home. But I'd felt that with the island house and the inside disappointed me. Fingers crossed that wouldn't happen here.

We walked up to the second story on the private outside staircase of the home. When Peg unlocked the door to let us in, I breathed a sigh of relief at seeing the welcoming hallway lined with white wainscoting. Coat hooks, a mirror, and a narrow bench were against the wall just inside the door.

From here, I could see into the sunny kitchen with its cream-colored cupboards and light beige quartz countertops. The apartment was emptied of furniture, but I could imagine my four counter stools, stored away in the moving pods shipped from California, pulled up against the island.

Peg took me on a tour of this floor of the historic home. "I'm not sure what was in this space originally, but when it was made into an apartment, great care was taken to keep original woodwork and built-ins." She showed me the ensuite bedroom, a second bedroom, and a hall bath. We then moved through the kitchen and dining area to the living room. Beautiful woodwork trimmed the cased opening into a small library lined with shelves. Perfect for an office for me. But what really caught my eye was the sunporch, with windows on three sides. From it, I stepped out onto a small balcony with a view across the bay.

"I'll take it!"

"Hooray," Peg shouted from inside the apartment. "I'm sure the landlady will be excited to hear this. You'll be the perfect tenant. I'm going to give her a call right now!"

To my left, my gaze took in the causeway and followed it out to Horseshoe Island and the Gulf of Mexico beyond it. A good pair of binoculars would be one of my first purchases because I love watching the sailboats gliding over the smooth waters. I looked back to the point where the causeway connected to the mainland. From here, I could see the river heading inland from the mouth of the Wimico River and the bustling marina and harbor area. Beyond the scope of my vision was the houseboat I'd been living in. And beyond that was the Shaw's River Lodge and Ella Winchester's homestead.

The park with the gazebo was down below me. The sounds of Saturday night long quieted, but a smile rose to my lips, thinking about what a perfect night of music and fireworks it had been. Now, young children were playing on the playground equipment and chasing after each other across the expanse of green grass. Beyond them, the River Road was busy with midweek traffic. The walking path was quiet now, but come early evening, the dog walkers would be out in force.

On my right, in the neighbor's yard, a young mother played with her toddlers in a game of hide and seek. It amused me to see how the little ones believed they could hide behind a light post. The mother played along, pretending not to see them even though they were hiding in plain sight.

Peg stepped out on the balcony to let me know the landlady was thrilled about me renting her apartment and looked forward to meeting me. "This has always been one of my favorite grand old ladies on the hill. It originally belonged to the Millers, one of the original logging families that helped build Seaside Cove."

"Just look at those little swashbucklers down there in the park. Like Tyler said, kids always romanticize pirates."

"They are so cute. And you'll have this amazing view to enjoy every day now. I'm so happy for you. There's a garage space for your car and a golf cart in the detached garage."

"Do you think it's okay to have my moving pods delivered here as soon as possible?"

"I'm sure Aubrey will be fine with that. You can sign the rental agreement at my office tomorrow. You're standing there looking out to the sea reminds me of how you looked coming into the harbor on Saturday, standing on the bow of the *Black Pearl*. That was the best capturing of our mayor scene I've ever been to." Peg suddenly pointed up toward the end of the island where the lighthouse stood. "Speak of the devil!"

It took me a minute to see what she was pointing toward. It was the *Black Pearl* with her sails unfurled, moving effortlessly over the calm waters. What a romantic image that made. The sleek black vessel sailing off toward adventures in South America. What would it be like to do something like that? This must be the same pull of the pirate lure as the young children felt. Was Damien a wealthy, accomplished man free to sail the world or a modern-day pirate? I held my head up into the breeze, imagining being the powerful and unafraid Grace O'Malley perched high up here, watching for enemies to enter the bay.

"Katie. Earth to Katie," Peg said, interrupting my pirate queen dream.

"Oops, sorry."

"It's okay," Peg said. "I was asking about what the inside of that yacht looked like. How many bedrooms? Do they have nice crew quarters, too? How about mounted fish hanging on the walls? Fully stocked kitchen?"

"Well, as to the number of bedrooms, I'm not sure, but there had to be generous crew quarters. It takes a lot of hands to sail a boat like that. And yes, a fully stocked kitchen along with a crew member who did double duty as a chef. I must admit I didn't see any mounted fish, but the place had stunning pieces of modern artwork, unusual sculptures, some antiques, and such. Just so much stuff you wouldn't expect to see on a boat."

"Wow! Off they go on another adventure. Gosh, but it must be thrilling to just set sail like that. They'll probably be sipping wine when the sun begins to sink on the horizon."

"I know I would if I was on there. But I'm here, and I'm happy I found my new home!"

CHAPTER FIFTEEN

Thursday morning, I went to Peg's office to sign the lease paperwork and put my deposit down. Then, I returned to my houseboat to continue packing there. The moving pods were scheduled for Friday afternoon delivery. Things were on track.

In the afternoon, I worked on the promotion and marketing for our Fourth of July event at the pub. If we could make the rooftop available for fireworks watching, it would be a big draw and would surely be an unusual event space. Definitely something to keep in mind for the future. In July, we'd booked a baby shower, an anniversary celebration, and a graduation ceremony for an area school that graduates emergency services students.

I made myself a quick sandwich before heading out

for a brisk walk to meet up with Aunt Maeve so we could walk together to Eve Brooks' house for our monthly book club meeting. Aunt Maeve had been taking more walks and getting more exercise, and I was always glad to join her.

My new apartment was just a few doors from Eve's, so I took Maeve over to show her where I would be living. She eagerly pointed out the variety of plants in the lush landscaping. "Ah, this place'll be bloomin' year-round with the grand selection of plants. What a lucky find this was for you. And for us! It's only a wee stroll from us and from the pub. Can't wait to have a peek inside. Will your California furniture work in there?"

"Much of it will, but I'll add some coastal cottage pieces after I get settled in. This view is extra special from the second floor. I'm excited to shop for wicker pieces for the sunroom."

Inside Eve's house, the rest of the club members were enjoying sparkling wine and light appetizers.

Peaches greeted me excitedly. "Katie, I just found out that the old Miller house's second-floor apartment is available! My friend's sister had been renting it for years and she couldn't do the stairs anymore, so she's getting a place at the retirement village. Are you still looking for a place?"

"I looked at that yesterday, Peaches. And I'm going to rent it."

"That's wonderful to hear. You'll be in our neighborhood now," Eve said. "And tonight, I'd like to welcome Winnie Stanley to our book club. I'm sure she's going to add a new dimension to our discussion."

"Thank you," Winnie said with her head held up proudly. "I read the book y'all told me to, so I'm all ready to add that dimension!"

"Will you miss the houseboat living?" Marge asked me.

"Sure, I will. I love the nighttime swamp critter voices and the soft sounds of the river rolling against the shore. Kind of reminds me of our novel for this month, *Where the Crawdads Sing*. But this week I got to visit another place that also reminded me of where Kya lived. Ella Winchester's home."

"Why on earth were you out there?" Winnie spit out. "All by herself out in the woods. Phew, not for me."

"Barbara wanted to see her and needed help to get there," I said, confused by Winnie's reaction. "Ella did a tarot reading for her on Saturday and then, after Bernie's death, she had some questions left for Ella and wanted to visit her."

"She's a strange one," Loretta said, shaking her head

slowly. "Sad story about a fire and losing her family. Turned her into a loner."

"More like an antisocial recluse, if you ask me," Winnie snapped back in a scornful tone.

"Like Kya, Ella is very self-reliant and has a deep affinity with nature. You should see the artwork she's created using pieces of nature. It was hanging on the willow arch over the path and in the trees around her yard. Reminded me of the movie and book too, with Kya's own passion for sketching birds and her mother's paintings of nature."

Winnie blurted out, "More like voodoo stuff, probably. All that mumbo jumbo and cards with old weird drawings on them. I leave all that alone. No, ma'am, none of that conjuring witch stuff for this old fat lady."

"Aye, Winnie, don't be a scaredy cat about such things," Maeve scolded. "I've never met the woman, but she's no witch. Look how everyone in Kya's world treated her, and she weren't nothing but a frightened and lonely child."

"Well, let's get going on our discussion of the book," Vivian Trimble, our former mayor's wife, said with of tone of impatience. This was the first book club meeting she'd been to since her husband was murdered.

"But wait, just a moment," Loretta said. "Does anyone have updates on the murder of that Green guy?"

Hannah offered up the fact that Darnell had taken drug-sniffing dogs to Bernie's boat, but they did not give an alert for drugs. "I've been trying to get any new information to report out of the police department, but they've been pretty tight-lipped."

"Drugs! The Green boy's father and mother would roll over in their graves if they thought that was going on," Loretta said.

"Don't know about that, as the Greens once got caught smuggling alcohol from the islands during prohibition. A matter of pick your poison, I say. But the family is familiar with crime," Marge added. "And isn't that what you were saying your next book is about? Some crime thriller involving dangerous characters. Like cartel members or something?"

"It is. Greg is pulling up some frightening statistics in his research," Eve said. "But in my novel, the bad guys lose…spoiler alert. In fact, Greg and I had what I consider an interesting idea. Those wicked, lawbreaking Greens of the past used the caskets to circumvent detection. We have an appointment tomorrow to tour their casket manufacturing facility in Woodville for a little research."

"Drugs are poisoning our youth," Peaches pronounced.

"Agreed," Loretta said. "A scourge on entire communities. Glad we don't see much of it here. But it's scary to think about smugglers starting to use our beautiful shore to bring in bad things."

"Okay, enough of all this," Eve said. "Let's get our conversation about *Where the Crawdads Sing* started."

When Maeve and I left later, there were lights on in the ground floor of my new home. I was goose-bumped all over again.

CHAPTER SIXTEEN

Sometime during the night, a thought popped into my head. As soon as I woke up in the morning, I contacted Eve and asked if I could tag along on her Woodville Casket Company tour. "You could call me your assistant."

"Sure, Katie. I'd love your company. But why would you want to visit a casket factory on a lovely day like this? Might it have something to do with the Green murder?" Eve's voice held a hint of mystery.

"It might," I said. "I'll talk to you on our ride out there. It's about an hour away, right? How about you pick me up at the pub, and I'll supply coffee from the Coffee Corner for you and Greg?"

"Now that sounds like a great idea. See you soon."

* * *

The Woodville Casket Company headquarters were down a gravel road off of the two-lane highway that took us into the town of Woodville. The cement block walls of the building were plain and unadorned except for the weathered sign reading Home of the Famous Woodville Caskets…Quality Caskets Since 1915. A few open windows lined the side of the building, and a large metal overhead door stood open to catch the breeze. The flat roof sprouted industrial air vents and chimneys. We parked near the door marked Visitor's Entrance, away from the employee parking lot where pickup trucks and dusty cars were lined up.

The waiting area was modest and drab, with four dark orange Naugahyde chairs, an end table, its laminate surface chipped in the corners, and a brochure rack filled with price and description sheets for the products being made here. But the smile of the front desk woman brightened the entire area.

"I can't believe I'm meeting such a famous author," she gushed, reaching for a book from her cluttered desk. "I just love your books. When I heard you were comin' I brought one along. Would you autograph this please?"

"Of course. Who shall I dedicate it to?"

"To Earleen. I just love your writing. Oh, I said that

already. Can I get a selfie with you, too? If it's not too much bother?"

A gruff male voice spoke loudly, startling us all. "Earleen!"

Earleen grimaced as Eve turned to see who had spoken. The spindly man with his shiny bald head and thick glasses gave Earleen the stink eye.

"It's quite alright. I don't mind at all," Eve said to him in her formal Southern lady accent.

"And you are?"

"We have an appointment to tour your facility this morning. I believe a Mr. Ortega was to show us around. I'm Evelyn Brooks. This is my co-author Greg and my assistant Katie."

"I didn't authorize this, and Mr. Ortega is busy at the moment," the man replied.

"We booked it," Greg said, his fingers sliding on his phone. "Here are the emails confirming it. We've come a long way. Is there someone else who could show us around?"

"No. We're very busy now."

As the man spun to leave, a woman walked out from one of the back offices. "What's going on, Terry?"

It was Victoria Ingalls, and she seemed to recognize me but then noticed Eve. "Why Eve Brooks! What on earth are you doing way out here? I haven't seen you since we served on the hospital board many moons ago."

"Oh my gosh. That really was a long time ago. I saw your boat in the parade on Saturday and kept an eye out for you at the festival. Sorry, I missed catching up with you there."

"I wasn't feeling well, and we left the festivities early," Victoria said. "But now I can personally tell you I'm in awe of your success, my friend! I see your books in all the stores."

"Research for my next book is the reason I'm here today, but why are you here, Victoria?"

"You haven't heard? This is all mine now. I am the proud owner of a casket company. Woo-hoo! Right?" Victoria's voice dripped with sarcasm as her fingers flicked on the worn surface of the receptionist desk.

"Ah, yes. I heard something to that effect, but I didn't put it together with you actually coming out here to work."

"Wish I didn't have to be here." Victoria shuddered. "But I must. Now, back to you. What are you researching?"

Eve's eyes flicked toward Terry before she turned to smile at Victoria. "I made an appointment last week, before the tragedy on the weekend, to tour the facility to check out specifics on how caskets are put together. But it appears communications got mixed up somewhere along the line."

"Terry, I don't see any reason why these people can't take a tour," Victoria spoke in a calm but authoritative voice.

"Ortega is busy, ma'am. And I don't like strangers in the factory. This ain't no tourist stop. There's insurance and liability. All that stuff."

"Nonsense, Terry," Victoria said. Her stern look made his teeth clench and his fists ball before he spun on his heels and stormed away without another word.

Victoria straightened her shoulders and adjusted the edge of her blouse. "As you can tell, my presence is not warmly embraced here. But Eve, if you don't expect a lot of specifics, I'd be happy to take you myself. Would be a nice break from pouring over the sad state of affairs with our accountant. Now, where do I know you from, young lady?"

"I'm Katie Murphy. Damien introduced us on Sunday morning at the marina."

"Ah, yes. A life-changing morning for all of us," Victoria said as she started down the drab hallway.

Greg reached around to extend his hand to Victoria as we followed her. "I'm Eve's son, Greg. We'll take you up on that offer. I'm sure if we have specific questions, we could just ask one of the other employees."

Victoria pushed through two large swinging doors at the far end of the hall. Inside the factory, the clanging of hammers and saws could be heard as workers constructed and assembled caskets. The faint sound of machinery whirring was accompanied by the clanging of metal tools and the beeping of a forklift. The air inside the plant was heavy with the scent of freshly cut wood, sawdust, and varnish, along with the faint smell of oil and grease from the machinery. Natural light, pouring through the high windows, highlighted the rows of unfinished wooden caskets that lined the production floor.

"Sorry about Terry's rudeness out there. I know he's not happy about me taking over," Victoria said. "Neither am I. Bernie and I were very hands off the business these last years."

"Is he the current plant manager?" Eve asked.

"Yes. But I'm coming to understand that he carries that title due more to seniority and familial connection than to ability. Come this way, and I'll have one of our employees give you a brief explanation of the process."

We stopped in front of what looked like a nearly completed casket, where a young man was working. He introduced himself as Sean and ran through the basics. Of all of us, Greg took the most interest in the actual process of manufacturing the caskets, especially the part where he discovered that the steel bed height of the interior was adjustable to allow for easier viewing.

"This is the perfect hiding spot," he said to me as Sean demonstrated the adjustability. "By using the adjustable feature to raise and lower the viewing mattress, which at the point of any sort of inspection would have been covered with a sheet and shirred crepe material that inspectors would have been hesitant to disrupt, they could have concealed the alcohol."

Victoria burst out laughing. "So that story is really true? Fred and Bernie were apparently so embarrassed by the great big family secret they didn't talk about it. But I'm starting to think they were the only ones still keeping it."

"And for our purposes, decades later, drugs could be hidden and smuggled in the same way," Eve said.

Other staff seemed uncomfortable around Victoria and our group. It had to be difficult for her, trying to figure things out here and becoming a hands-on boss so suddenly and knowing she was making plans to sell. I'm sure Sean would be asked a lot of questions at his lunch break.

Terry lurked back in the dark corners of the plant, watching us as he talked on his cell phone. Victoria noticed him, too, because she quickly wrapped up our tour and said that Earleen would see us out before she strode angrily in Terry's direction.

"Now that was abrupt," Eve said. "She looks super stressed. I remember her from when she was married to Bernie and lived in Seaside Cove, but that was a very long time ago. A lot of water under the bridge since then. Do you two want to grab some lunch? I'm starved."

When we pushed through the swinging doors back into the lobby, we overheard a nervous Earleen speaking on the phone. "Yes, sir, I understand. But she allowed it." A pause, then, in an even more flustered tone, Earleen said, "No, I don't think they...yes. Sure." She waved goodbye to us and mouthed a thank you to Eve. I hung back a step and heard her say, "They are leaving now, sir."

CHAPTER SEVENTEEN

As soon as we were settled into the booth at the diner just up the road, Eve said, "I feel we got a good sense of the place. This was well worth the trip, don't you agree, Greg?"

"Sure do. I've done online research, but to put yourself right in the middle of the smells and sounds of a place like that makes a big difference. The idea of using the coffins to smuggle drugs further into the country is perfect." Greg looked up at the waitress, who had appeared at our table.

She looked like a woman of the world who'd seen a lot in her lifetime, but still, her eyes popped wide open at Greg's words. So much so that I felt I should explain what he was talking about. I caught the name on her tag and said, "Linda, let me explain Greg's words."

"Well, miss, no need to worry 'bout my opinion. Just here to take your order."

Eve realized how it must have sounded also, so she helped me out. "We just got done visiting the Woodville Casket Company. I'm an author and was doing research for my next crime thriller about the criminal under-world of drug cartels. I had the idea of using caskets to smuggle drugs deep into other states. My son's remarks were regarding that idea. Do you think that would be believable?"

Linda raised her pen to her lips. "Well, now, ma'am, I reckon that could happen. Why not? Those coffins are hauled all round the United States. Just ask Roy there. He's been pickin' up at Woodville for a long time." She pointed her pen toward a man sitting at the diner counter. He was hunched over his coffee cup with a book propped on the napkin holder in front of him. "And he's a reader. Might know who you are, ma'am. Now, can I get that order so's you can get somethin' in your tummies?"

Apparently, Linda had mentioned us to Roy because as we finished our lunch, he ambled over to us, his hat in hand. "Linda says you're an author who writes crime thrillers. That's my favorite read. Could I ask your name in case I know your books?"

"Certainly, Roy, sit down a minute. I write as the author E.L. Brooks. Does that sound familiar to you?"

Roy humbly lowered his head and pulled a chair up from a nearby table, his rough hands gripping the edges tightly. "Well, I'll be danged. Sure, I know you."

"Are you surprised about me being a woman?"

"No, ma'am. Easy to tell you're a right classy woman."

Eve chuckled at the misinterpretation of her question. "I'm sorry. I meant to ask if you're surprised that the author E.L. Brooks is a woman."

Roy slapped himself upside the head with a laugh. "Got me there. Yep, I guess I am. Does that make me any of those incorrect thinker people?"

"Not at all," Eve said with a wink. "It makes me wise to use initials, so the readers don't know and don't care. Linda told us you drive big rigs to deliver Woodville caskets all over the United States. Do you have time to answer a couple of questions? Research for the book."

"Not at all. I'd be right proud to say I helped you research, ma'am." The flabbergasted grin on his face quickly faded. "But I'm kind of tied up waitin' for a call from Terry over at the plant that my load is all wrapped up and ready for pickup."

"I'll be quick then. Is Woodville a well-respected brand?" Eve asked.

"Well, let me tell you somethin'. Those caskets from

Woodville ain't like others I've seen. They're sturdy as an oak tree, and ain't nobody fallin' out of 'em, no sir."

The diner had cleared out by this time, and Linda stopped by to see if we wanted more coffee.

"Ain't that right, Linda?" Roy asked her.

"Yes, sir. Woodville's are the best. Not like that cheap old thing Billy Bob's kids got for him." With a stifled chuckle, she regaled us with a humorous tale recounting the time when the bottom of a casket suddenly broke loose as it was being carried from the church to the waiting hearse.

"Now, get this picture in your heads. They was carryin' his coffin to the hearse. The first pall bearer plopped the casket down in the back of the vehicle, ready to slide it on in. Lord have mercy, I reckon they might still be using that old hearse. But anyways, right before them fellas were gonna let go of their handles and slide Billy Bob in the rest of the way, there was a loud crack, and the bottom gave out. And wouldn't ya know it, Billy Bob's feet came slippin' out. Boy, you shoulda heard the hollerin' and wailin' that went round."

We all broke out in laughter. I almost spit out my coffee!

"Did he get put back in?" Roy asked, eagerly leaning forward to hear her answer.

"Sure did, and right smooth they were about it. The

back two fellas lifted the separating bottom panel at the narrow back end of the box, and sort of bounced it up a couple times so's Billy Bob slid back into place. I never did hear what they did at the grave site though." Linda snorted softly. "That story grew legs 'round here all right. Sure weren't no Woodville product."

"Another quick question Roy, are you aware of any irregularities going on at the plant?" Eve asked. 'Have you heard one of the owners just passed away? We all live in Seaside Cove, where his brother Frederick Green lives."

Roy looked surprised and glanced at Linda as though looking for confirmation from her to speak. She nervously licked her lips before telling him to go ahead.

He leaned in closer, lowering his voice conspiratorially. "Funny you should ask. I gotta tell ya, there's been some strange things going on with them lately. I've talked to Linda here about it cause she knows a lot of the guys that work there. Lately, I've been makin' deliveries at these warehouses in the middle of nowhere or in odd places at the edge of cities. They ain't my usual delivery spots if you catch my meaning. I get my routing all set up, bills of lading in order, then after I'm on the road, I get a phone call that the drop-off location changed. Just out of the blue."

"How long has this been going on?" Greg asked.

Roy's eyes narrowed in concentration. "Close on a year now, if I recall right. I don't question why. I just follow orders."

"And Terry is the man who requests those changes?" I didn't want to put words in his mouth, but I needed the information.

"Yep. He does all that stuff." A ringtone of guitar chords rang out. "And there he is now. My load must be ready to pick up. Nice meeting ya' all."

Greg's brow furrowed. "What is that song?"

"I Walk the Line by Johnny Cash," I answered.

"Now, how does a youngin' like you know that?" Linda asked in a skeptical voice.

"He's big in Ireland, too," I said with a grin. "Ready to hit the road? I've got to get back to Seaside for a party tonight."

CHAPTER EIGHTEEN

Following the road trip and tour of the casket factory, where we were surrounded by dust and fumes, I made the decision to freshen up with a shower before heading to the pub for the evening. The shower had always been a place for me to think.

My mind wandered back to the truck driver's answer to my question about Terry. The question came up because of what Barbara had told me about Bernie wanting to check out some things while he was in town. Could Terry have been on Bernie's mind? At first, I doubted changes in delivery locations warranted examination by Bernie, but the way Roy described it, they were unusual for him. I wished Roy hadn't been called away because his load was ready. I would have liked to ask him more.

I tucked my thoughts back in my mind to enjoy the good feeling of anticipation for a laid-back Friday night with Blaire and her friends at the pub. They had reserved the corner section of the pub for the bachelorette party, wanting to have their own space down here with the public rather than using an upstairs area.

My idea of offering a package for smaller parties like these had taken off. We got commitments on food, usually finger food appetizers, and our local bakery supplied the cutest cupcakes in whatever colors were appropriate. In this instance, I knew the colors were soft greens and lavender.

The place was busy, but Blaire's party group hadn't yet arrived. Though someone had come in earlier to do a setup of a banner, balloons, and various playful decorations. This type of thing was what I loved about being here and being part of Uncle Paddy's dream. I'd been to bachelorette parties in Las Vegas, Cabo San Lucas, and I'd even been the party planner for a weekend-long one in Palm Springs. I'd seen the spectrum. But this low-key vibe of just getting together would be just as much fun as any of those.

Most of the people here would know at least one of the partygoers. They'd love seeing them celebrating the upcoming marriage, along with throwing out some of their own good-hearted teasing and fun for the bride-to-be.

Jack and Sophia were having a drink at the bar. "What a nice surprise to see you two back in town so soon," I said. "Just for the weekend?"

"Yep, our realtor, Peg, has a few more places to show us," Sophia said. "She's so patient with this process. And we love having the excuse to get away from the city for the weekend."

"She just helped me find an apartment to rent," I said. "I'm super excited about it."

"Good to hear. I look forward to seeing it," Jack said. He went on to tell me that he was going to talk with Darnell about what his questions at the agency had led him to discover and thanked me for suggesting he look into the situation.

On my way to the bar to get a drink, I stopped at a table to greet Tim Douglas. "Glad to see you got out of pirate prison."

Tim's grin widened as he flexed his muscles. "Powered my way out! I've never had such a great time at a pirate festival before. I can't believe how much money the town raked in." He gestured towards the booth where Fred and Fran were sitting. "Fred just gave me the final figures. The dunk tank alone made double what it did last year, and we had twice as many vendors paying to participate."

It made me happy to see Fred out and about again. I ordered a Guinness from Liam and waved hello to Paddy, who was at the far end of the bar, before making my way to the Green's booth, where I noticed Barbara was with them. So, she'd stuck to her word to stay in town.

"Hi all. Nice to see you getting out on a Friday night."

"No wakes today," Fran said. "Though we're always sort of on call, you might say."

"Mayor Tim just told me about the financial success of the festival. I'm glad you've got that treasurer duty out of your hair," I said.

"It surpassed my expectations," Fred said, a hint of pride lacing his words. "This is the third year I've been treasurer, and we exceeded in every category." It was a relief to see him back to his old self, full of enthusiasm and optimism. I couldn't help but feel happy for him.

Barbara slid further over, closer to the wall, and patted the booth seat next to her. "Please join us for a moment, Katie. We've just been talking about something you might be interested in hearing."

As soon as I'd taken my seat, Fred leaned in to speak. "Barbara and I have been comparing notes about my dear departed brother. Besides his being an astute businessman, he was also a big-hearted, fun-loving guy."

"And that's part of what the tarot card signaled," Barbara said. "On Tuesday Ella put me properly in my place, explaining she was not a fortune teller but a person who intuits. She remembered the specifics of the cards I drew from her that day. It helped me a great deal to better understand the man I loved."

Fred visibly blushed and reached across the table for Barbara's hand. "He really cared for you. And certainly, as much more than a neighbor. By his very own words, he expressed his wish to straighten out the business again, get it on the profitable side, and then be free to travel the seas with you."

A tear glistened in Barbara's eye. "I believe that now. And I love you for telling me about your conversation with him while I was getting my cards read. That meant the world to me."

Fred turned back to address me directly. "When I sat with Bernie right in this spot last Saturday, he explained that he wanted to enjoy the weekend before tackling the problems at the factory. My brother was homing in on what he called suspicious activity at the Woodville Casket Company." Fred's voice cracked when he asked, "He did have a blast on Saturday, didn't he, Barbara?"

"He sure did."

Fran spoke, "Okay, you two, back to the business thing. Katie, these two soft-hearted but gotta love 'em folk have put their heads together and realized just how many irregularities in production and accounting have been found."

"Found where?" I asked, already suspecting what the answer would be.

"At Woodville Casket Company," Fred said. "When Barbara was allowed back on the *Cruising Along* to get her personal belongings, she also picked up Bernie's briefcase and laptop and brought them to me. She knew the code to get into the computer."

"He let me use it when we traveled," Barbara quickly explained. "I'd never ever go nosing into his business records. But he'd been pouring over them on the way here, and I thought Fred, knowing numbers and data like he does, what with being treasurer for the festival and running his own business, should have access to them."

Fred's chest bumped out with pride. "The laptop contained the accounting and shipping system used at the factory, and he'd flagged certain things. When I delved in deeper, I, too saw the anomalies and discrepancies. In his briefcase, he had a handwritten list, spelling out specific questions he wanted to bring up when he visited the plant."

"I think Fred should take these things to Victoria since she will be taking over the factory once Bernie's estate is settled," Fran said. "I'm of the mind he shouldn't worry or concern himself about it at this point. What's happened is done. It's not his problem now. Let her figure it out."

Fred shifted uncomfortably in the booth seat. "And I'm feeling like I'm sticking my nose where it shouldn't be. Those are private papers, after all."

"Not private. They are part of the business, and since you're executor of your brother's estate, you have a right to see them. But now you saw them!" Fran pounded her fist on the table. "Pass them on to Victoria, or her lawyer, or Bernie's lawyer, or whoever's lawyer, and forget about it!"

"Do you think Darnell should be given this information, too?" Barbara asked me. "I only got it late yesterday after he called me to say I could go on the boat and get my things. Could it have something to do with the murder? Like maybe someone at the plant trying to cheat Bernie and Victoria? Financial fraud? Embezzlement?"

"Good thought, Barbara. If there was something fishy going on at his business, it definitely could be a motive for murder. And to see the issues with the plant would be important," I said. Taking in this new information and putting it together with what I'd seen and heard earlier today, I felt they were on to something. I took a moment to explain the trip to the plant. How it came up as a research trip for Eve's newest book. "Victoria was there and mentioned going over things with the accountant. I agree with Fran. You should give this paperwork and stuff to her, but not until after Darnell's had a chance to see it."

No one spoke, but Fred and Barbara looked at each other.

"What?" I said. "You don't think that's a good idea?"

"Well…let me put it this way. A little birdie told me…" Fred was interrupted by the appearance of his ex-sister-in-law and her husband.

"Well, look at this, will ya? Here we are all together. Richard, I'm not sure if you met the special friend of my ex. Brenda…oops, Barbara…I'm sorry, I never got your last name, dear."

"Werner."

"Werner," Victoria turned to repeat it to Richard. "And I don't know if I mentioned it to you, darling, but Katie Murphy here was at the Woodville Casket plant today. Isn't that odd? What a funny thing to run into you twice in one day."

Richard was obviously the more sober of the two. "It's nice to meet you Barbara, and good to see you again, Katie. Fred, I didn't get to extend my condolences to you and Fran. Now come along, Victoria, we've interrupted their conversation."

"Nonsense!" Victoria burped and gave us an uncomfortably awkward grin. "We're all one big happy family here in Seaside, aren't we? Everybody knows everybody. I gotta tell ya' Katie, I'm sorry you were treated so rudely by Terry Green. He's not the most pleasant… oops." Victoria snorted and covered her mouth. "He's a cousin of yours, Fred, isn't he? But then I guess you've heard that before because when I was married to Bernie, he was made out to be the black sheep of the family…or was it a goat? Haha." She put her finger to her chin and squinted her eyes in concentration. "Hmm…wait. Didn't he go to jail for a while? Oh, my memory is going downhill fast. Anyway, I think his head might be on the chopping block."

Yikes, had she been hitting the bottle since I saw her this afternoon? Probably the stress of dealing with everything this week has gotten to her. I knew I wanted to make my exit to join the bachelorette party, so I slipped out of the booth and around Victoria and Richard. Fred didn't get to tell me what that little birdie told him, but that would have to wait.

CHAPTER NINETEEN

Blaire's friends varied in height, weight, hair color, and style in every way possible. But the common denominator among them all was the soft green and lavender T-shirts they wore. And the saying on the shirts cracked me up. They all started with most likely to…followed by a variety of funny sayings… dance on tables, keep the party going, get us all arrested, go home early! The person who obviously was the bride wore a veil, and her T-shirt read most likely to get hitched. What an introduction to the group. I wondered what my T-shirt would have said.

Blaire ran to greet me. "I'm so glad you're here, Katie. I can't wait for you to meet my friends. And thank you for seeing to the food and letting us bring in decorations ahead of time. Come on over here and meet Maddie. She's the bride-to-be."

And off I went, swept up in meeting Blaire's friends. I was quickly welcomed into the gathering and soaked up the chatter and laughter. They all appeared to be about the same age, and I soon learned many had been friends since high school. The live musicians began to play, and everyone, and I mean everyone in the pub joined in singing or dancing, especially with Maddie.

I noticed Paddy come over and greet one of the partygoers, a woman with a ready smile and dark hair in a flattering mid-length cut before he ordered their waitress to bring a round of drinks on him. Then he brought her over to me. "Katie, meet Aubrey. By all accounts, we're lucky to have her on as our new accountant. Pun intended!"

"Hey, Katie. I'm glad we finally got to meet. Your uncle speaks highly of what you've done to help build up Paddy's Pub. And by the way, you did a bang-up job for our friend's party. And I even noticed your music tonight is perfect for our age! Nice touch!"

"Thanks much, Aubrey. I'm glad Blaire invited me to join in with all of you." The feeling of being part of this group of friends was like a warm embrace, something I'd been missing since moving here.

"Oh, and by the way, I'm thrilled we're going to be

close neighbors," Aubrey said with a wink. "You'll be right above me!"

Excitement tingled through me, as though I'd just found a hidden treasure. "I thought your name sounded familiar! You're Aubrey Miller? And that's your house I'm renting in? I love it! Here I had the landlady pictured as…ahh…maybe like a generation older than you?"

Paddy said, "Well, if that ain't grand. Katie's already been packing things up to move into her new place. So now it appears that you are going to be a big part of our life, Aubrey."

Aubrey and I hit it off immediately. She explained that she inherited the house from her great-aunt. "The second floor had been made into an apartment years ago. The rental income helped my great-aunt keep the place up. When she passed, and I took over, I updated the apartment and kept the same renter for over five more years. But the stairs got to be too much for her, and she moved to the old folk's home."

"Your renter was a friend of one of the ladies in my book club. She told me about it last night."

"Wow! Small world. Oh, and your pods have arrived." Aubrey clapped to get everyone's attention. "Hey guys, guess who's gonna live above me?" She pointed at me, and a cheer rose up from the girls. "Who's up for helping her move some things tomorrow?"

"I'll volunteer Sean," Maddie said. "He's staying in town tonight with Josh. Maybe both of them will be willing to help."

"My brother could help out, too," a blonde wearing the most likely to keep the party going T-shirt offered.

"That would be great," I said. "Liam offered to show up, so we should be able to move it all in one day."

"Liam, as in that hunky bartender of yours?" Blaire asked. "I'll be there for sure!"

Laughter followed as all of us turned to look toward the bar. Liam, surprised by the sudden attention, gave us a wave from behind the bar. He was a big plus here. Not only was he authentically Irish and a cousin of some sort to me, but he was also a big draw with the younger crowd. He could talk sports with all the men, and his impish grin was welcomed by the ladies.

"Katie, could I take the girls upstairs and show them the room I'm thinking of using for our reception?" Maddie asked after a long session on the dance floor. "I could use a break."

"Sure, come on, I'll go with you."

As we climbed the staircase, Blaire said, "This place is amazing. This woodwork must be original. And just look at these black and white photographs. My mom teased me about Molly McCracken's ghost still haunting this place."

"I've heard that before, too. I think she's in one of these photos."

Maeve had shown Maddie the rooms back in March and booked the event in our calendar, so she knew the basics about opening up the wide double doors to form a bigger event space. But I went on to explain how easily we could set up a DJ and dance floor. Maddie and I made plans to meet up in a couple of weeks to finalize things.

As we all headed back down to the pub, I excused myself to use the bathroom up here. But before I could step in, I heard voices. Sounded like two people arguing, and one of them was a man. What was he doing in the women's restroom? I decided to give them a minute. I didn't want to step into the middle of it.

The man's voice, low and controlled, said, "Calm down. I'll give him a good talking to."

Then, a woman replied with a familiar-sounding slur in her voice, "No. He's out. Ain't no family of mine. And I want out, too. Period. Sell. The place is a money pit."

"Soon, I promise. Okay? We'd be selling at a loss now. Just give it a chance."

"We?" Then louder. "We? Me, you mean. My decision. I'm going back downstairs."

I ducked into one of the dark banquet rooms as Victoria stormed down the hall and headed for the staircase, Richard close on her heels. I waited until they were safely past before I stepped back out and peered down the open railing to see them leave the pub.

Richard tried to take Victoria's arm, but she yanked it away before pushing past our mannequin Mel and out the front door, almost tripping over the stoop before someone caught her. It was Jesse. After making sure Richard had hold of Victoria, Jesse entered the pub, where I lost sight of him.

I stepped into the restroom to do my business, which now included putting on some fresh lipstick. An expensive tube of Chanel lipstick lay open on the bathroom counter. It had to be Victoria's since pub guests don't normally use this restroom. What were they doing up here? Maybe the one downstairs had been busy. I grabbed the tube, closed it up and tucked in my jeans, then headed back down to the party.

Jesse was getting a drink at the bar and talking with Liam and Paddy before he came across the room toward our party, skirting his way around the dance floor. He came over and put his arm around the shoulder of the cute blonde in our group. Now I remembered seeing her before. She'd been with Jesse at a brunch here back in January.

"Ready to go?" he asked her.

"Sure, but first, I have to make sure you can help

with something tomorrow. My new friend Katie needs help to move some furniture, and I volunteered you."

"You did now, did you?" Jesse gave me a knowing smile. "I'd like to think she's my friend, too."

"You know each other?"

"Yes, we do, sis. And I'd be happy to help. In fact, I would consider it a pleasure."

The pleasure is all mine, I thought!

CHAPTER TWENTY

I was up bright and early on Saturday morning. Since the houseboat had come furnished, I'd been without my own furniture for months now. It would feel wonderful to see my own things again today.

The three big orange moving pods were waiting on the side drive near the private entry stairs to my new apartment. I carried the padlock keys and opened each of the doors on the pods. Welcome home possessions... time to move you in!

I grabbed a small box to take up the stairs with me. Something just to say I have landed. When I opened it, I discovered it contained my framed photographs. I immediately unpacked them and put them on a shelf in what would be my office.

The morning sun spilling in through the faceted

glass transom windows of the small library created prisms of color that bounced around the room. A knock at a door somewhere just outside this room startled me. But then I realized it had to be Aubrey. There must be an inside staircase. Of course, this used to be part of the original house.

"Come on in!" I called out.

"Unlock the door," she called back.

"Oh, sorry." I tried one door, and it opened to a coat closet. Then the next one I tried looked like it was a small narrow staircase, probably to an attic space. Behind the third door was my landlady, holding a tray of bottled water, fresh fruit, and granola bars.

"Welcome, neighbor! Thought I'd put these out for now, and we can order pizza later." She laughed and handed me the tray, delighting in my surprise. "I'll be right back up. I forgot the toilet paper, soap, and hand towels I'd gotten to get you started here."

And with that, she was gone down the back staircase. I put the tray on my kitchen counter and the drinks in the refrigerator.

Soon, I heard Aubrey returning. She made a dash for the hall bath to put the essentials in it and popped back out. "There. We're ready for the helpers' arrival. I have coffee on downstairs. Want to come down and see my place?"

"I'd love to. It's terrific that these mansions on the hill have been kept up so well."

"It was a bit of scandal when Aunt Gertrude put an apartment on the second floor. There goes the neighborhood and all that. But she was running out of money to keep this grand old lady in good shape by herself, so a boarder seemed the best answer for her."

"Makes sense, but why would the neighbors care?" I asked.

"Old mansions broken up into apartments? Doesn't always go well for neighborhoods. It can be a slippery slope. Next thing you know, the upkeep of the homes starts going down. Cars parking on the street. Piles of kids' toys in the yard. Dogs and cats living together."

A totally spontaneous laugh escaped me. "I understand now. You can't have that! Does anyone complain about your next-door neighbor with kids?"

"The one with the kid's toys in her yard? She's a local attorney. Her two kids can be a handful, but she manages. Her husband is some sort of financial guy and travels a lot. Plus, they pick up after the little ones." Aubrey opened the door to the staircase, but before we started down, she stopped. "I'm warning you! You'll be shocked at how much old lady stuff I've kept. Don't judge!"

As I turned on the final landing to the front hall, the

site literally took my breath away. My eyes scanned the entryway, taking in the multiple framed artwork and photographs hanging on every square inch of wall space, except where an intricately carved hall table stood with a stained-glass lamp on it. A brass-monkey statue, along with several other unique pieces, covered much of the narrow table's surface.

"My aunt was quite a character," Aubrey said as I peered closely at the intricate details of what the monkey was holding. "I think that came from China. She said the monkey was her zodiac animal, or she was born in the year of the monkey? I forget."

"And she collected things," I said. "Like butterflies in the shadow boxes. I'm overwhelmed, to be honest. But also, super curious."

"Good. I love that in people," Aubrey said, leading me down the hall, past several cased openings and numerous doorways. We ended up in the kitchen.

"This I redid immediately. I love to cook and bake, so it was my first priority."

The gleaming appliances, creamy cabinets with soft beige quartz countertops, and the big island somehow looked familiar.

"Yes, they are the same cabinets as the ones upstairs," she said as she poured me a cup of coffee from her typical coffee maker. A modest, ordinary kitchen appliance. But next to it stood an espresso machine, close to the size of our commercial one in the Coffee Corner.

Aubrey noticed me taking it in. "One of my guilty pleasures is acquiring kitchen products and gadgets. Come on. Might as well give you evidence. Here's my pantry."

Again, my mouth dropped open. I'll be the first to admit I'm not into cooking and baking and stuff like that. So, I didn't even know what some of the things in her pantry were used for. She continued taking me around the first floor, including showing me her home office in what had been the original parlor.

"My uncle passed away long before Gertrude. She loved him and missed him but embraced widowhood seriously. Funny way to say it, but he never cared for travel, and they had no children, so she was off to see the world. And oh, the stories she brought back. They enthralled me as a young girl. Probably part of why I kept so many of these things she gathered while traveling the world."

"But doesn't it feel a little claustrophobic?" I asked.

With a big belly laugh, Aubrey said, "When I get that feeling, the urge to get something out of here because it's crowding me, or I don't want to dust the ancient African mask one more time, or I stub my toe on the lion's head table foot again, I pop online and scour the web. No bragging, but I know my way around the auction and antiques sites pretty well. You'd be surprised at the monetary value of some of this. Confidentially, I wonder how she got some of this stuff out of the country of origin. Don't even get me started with the attic. We'll save that for another day."

"Are you a traveler like her?" I asked.

"I've done some. Especially lately because of how easy it is to access my business accounts remotely. Things have changed so much since I began doing my freelance accounting. But not any travel close to what Gertrude did. At least not yet. How about you?"

"Well, I came here from Ireland years ago and have enjoyed a few trips in the United States. Mostly to get out of the hustle and bustle of the big city. I was a party planner in LA, and occasionally, it meant I took trips for that, too. When I lived in Ireland, I traveled around the UK and Europe. It was more like you travel between different states here."

"Lucky you. Ireland is on my travel bucket list," she said.

"Aren't we kind of young for bucket lists?" I asked.

"Never too young. If I knock off my top-line items, I'll just add in more at the bottom. I've never taken a cruise. That's another one. I've been sailing with friends around here on the Gulf, and sometimes on overnights, but I mean a big cruise like to Europe. Or one through the Panama Canal to South America."

"Did you see the *Black Pearl* in the boat parade last Saturday? It's on the way to the Panama Canal now."

"I sure did see it! Gorgeous! Was that you on the boat playing the woman pirate? It just hit me now. You looked amazing as a pirate lady."

I cleared my throat and puffed up my chest. "Pirate Queen is what I was. Grace O'Malley was a real person from Ireland."

Aubrey did a silly bow, and we ended up giggling again.

"Oops, sounds like the gang is here. Time to get to work!" Aubrey grabbed me by the arm. "Come along girlfriend, can't keep the help waiting."

CHAPTER TWENTY-ONE

With the help of everyone who showed up, the day sped by. The narrower staircase and doorways of the older home meant it took some creative shifting and tilting to get the larger pieces through, but the pods were emptied by early afternoon. Everyone even dug in and helped me unpack my boxes.

I had a few surprises. Maddie's future groom, Sean, was the very man who'd explained how the casket bed was raised up and down at the Woodville Casket Company yesterday. It turns out his friend Josh was the boat engine repair guy at the marina.

My cousin Liam had a great time hanging out and helping. Blaire and Aubrey were especially grateful he showed up, and he soaked up every bit of their atten-tion. It seemed his muscles did more flexing than required, but by the fixed grin on his face, I could tell he was loving it.

Jesse proved to be especially helpful as he brought along a tool chest in his ATV. Despite contradicting opinions of where things should be positioned on which wall, we managed to get most of my mirrors and wall hangings hung up. Plus, Jesse patiently put together the counter stools that had been disassembled for the move.

I gladly accepted Josh's offer to drive me back to my houseboat in his pickup so I could gather my things and be ready to stay here overnight. Josh seemed like a friendly, albeit slightly reserved person. It was hard to imagine him having any involvement with Bernie's death.

"Can I ask you something, Josh?" I said but quickly backtracked thinking he might consider me too invasive. "You don't have to answer if you don't want. You know I was there when you came to the harbor Sunday morning and talked to the chief of police. Later, from a different boat owner, I heard that there had been angry words between you and someone else. The man wasn't sure but thought it might have been the captain of *Cruising Along* or Bernard Green, the owner."

"Yeah, I remember seeing you there. I've been just sick thinking about the whole thing. Especially knowing people are talking about me being careless or negligent at my work. It feels so unfair."

I felt so bad for Josh. He had a target on him as he admitted he'd disconnected the batteries to work on the compressor. The question was if he'd failed to reinstall them.

"I didn't have an argument with anyone," Josh said. "The captain got a little hot because I arrived to fix the compressor later than I had promised. He was a very impatient person. But everything seemed fine when I called to let him know I had it up and running again."

"So that was Friday night, right?" I asked.

"It was."

"Josh, when you were working on the *Cruising Along* on Friday, did anyone stop and chat with you or seem nosy about what you were doing?" I had to press him about this. Who else knew that there was an issue with the compressor?

"The captain was there, obviously. And he was pushing me to finish up. But they were hooked up to shore power in the marina, so I wasn't sure why it was such a big deal until I got wind that the harbormaster, Lyle, was worried about the power draw being too great with the extra boats that would show up on Saturday. I heard a couple of boaters hanging out and talking with the captain about it. The captain said that's why he needed to get the bleeping compressor fixed cause his boss couldn't sleep without air conditioning in hot weather. Said some pretty derogatory things about Mr. Green."

"But you didn't know who specifically was talking about the electric power because you were in the engine room, right?"

"That's right. But it was a couple of other boat owners. I saw them at one point, but they had their backs to me. Look, I know you don't know me, but I heard about how you kinda helped with the mayor's murder a few months ago." A pained look crossed Josh's face as he pulled up to my houseboat and shut the truck off. "I know Darnell is an okay kind of policeman and will do the right thing. But I'm scared. I've never been in any mess like this in all my thirty-some years."

"Josh, you're right about the chief doing the right thing. And I've got a few things that have come onto my radar I'm going to share with him. If you could just mention any identifying features of the men talking with the captain, like height, weight, hair color, it might be helpful. And then I'll let you know if I hear anything new."

"Thanks, Katie. That means a lot." As we carefully packed my last few boxes and belongings onto the pickup, I couldn't help but feel a twinge of regret at leaving behind my home on the river. Not to fall asleep to the gentle lapping of water against the hull, the chorus of crickets and frogs in the evening, the occasional splash as a fish leaped out of the water. I took one last deep breath, imprinting the scent of the river air in my memory, then switched gears and told Josh we had pizzas to pick up and we'd better get going.

Everyone had gathered around Aubrey's backyard picnic table. Beer and wine, along with paper plates, parmesan cheese, and pepper flakes, were ready and waiting when Josh and I arrived with the fresh, hot pizzas.

Maddie and Sean's wedding plans were the first big topic of discussion. His bachelor party would happen in a couple of weeks and included renting lodging at Jesse's place on the river. Jesse's sister teased him about being the old man in this millennial group.

"Will you be babysitting the guys?" she said.

I caught Jesse giving me an eye roll. "I like to hang out with you children. Makes me feel younger by at least two years."

Sean wrapped his arm around Maddie. "At least we won't be dancing on tabletops for my party."

"Hey, we did no such thing! At least not that I saw." She giggled. "But it was a fun night. What are you guys going to do for your bachelor party?"

"We'll be catching fish. Cleaning fish. Eating fish," Jesse pantomimed the actions as he spoke. "Then repeating that the next day."

"Maybe a little beer drinking in between," Sean added. "Right, Josh?"

"I hope so," he said. "Maybe the police will have everything figured out by then so I can relax."

Everyone quieted and all eyes were turned toward Josh. He flushed with embarrassment and looked down.

Maddie asked, "What are they figuring out?"

When Josh didn't answer, Blaire, knowing what was happening because of her position in the police department, hesitantly spoke up. "You all didn't hear? Josh is sort of involved with that tragic incident of the guy dying in his boat last weekend."

A soft collective gasp sounded as they absorbed this startling information, but Josh's eyes remained fixed on the ground.

"We've got your back, buddy," Sean said. "They'll get it all sorted out."

"Hey man, don't let this get you down. Some people have nothing better to do than gossip," Liam added. "Believe me, I hear all kinds of garbage at my job."

"Speaking of the boat guy, he owned the casket place where I work," Sean said. "I wonder what's going to happen to that business. Katie, maybe you know about that woman who was showing you around the plant. I know she's one of the owners. What's going to happen now that her partner is dead?"

It seemed a good time to tell more of the story I'd filled in so far. These were good people who wanted to help their friend Josh, just like I did. "Victoria will be the sole owner. It was set up during their divorce. The company purchased life insurance to go to the heirs of whoever passed away first. The other partner would end up owning the entire company. Easier than trying to run a business with heirs of a dead partner."

"Why were you at the casket factory?" Jesse asked me.

"It's a little weird, but I became Eve Brooks' assistant for the day. She had this crazy idea about smuggling drugs in caskets for her next crime thriller."

"Whoa, that's an interesting idea," Aubrey said. "Very clever and original. I can see where Mrs. Brooks would be able to put that in one of her thrillers."

"Not as original as you might think," Sean said. "I've heard the stories about shipping liquor in the caskets during prohibition. It would come to Wimico Cove from islands like Jamaica. You all know the Rum Runner restaurant. That's where it got the name."

The millennials here didn't seem to know much about that history, so Jesse gave a colorful explanation of the prohibition era, including bathtub gin and speakeasies. He really seemed to know the history of that era, and everyone listened intently, even asking a few questions.

"Wow, thanks, Jesse, our wise and much older sage," Sean said. "Let's give him a round of applause."

"And there will be a test on this at your bachelor party, children." Jesse wagged his finger at them.

"Back to the smuggling. Sean, do you think Eve's idea would fly?" Blaire asked. "Could something ship illegally that way again?"

Sean shrugged and reached for another piece of pizza.

But Jesse spoke up, "I suppose it could. Why not?"

"Eww!" Maddie said. "Sean, you've never told me that story about the Greens being smugglers."

"Didn't I? It seemed sort of far-fetched. And way before I was even born." Sean's face grew serious. "But thinking about now...hmm. For over a year now, I've noticed someone comes into the building during off hours. Things have been moved, changed around."

"Be serious," Maddie scolded. "Ohh, maybe it's a ghost coming back because he didn't like the Woodville casket he was buried in."

Sean's expression made me feel he had been serious,

but Maddie's joke about it stopped him from saying more.

Hearing Maddie's joke about the ghost, I couldn't help but share the story that Linda had told me at the diner about Billy Bob's casket falling apart. It had everyone laughing as our gathering broke up. Jesse and Liam had to head to work. Maddie and Sean were driving back to Woodville tonight. Josh had a job to finish up. Aubrey and Jesse's sister left for a stroll along the river trail with Blaire, but I passed on their offer to join them. It had been an exciting but exhausting day, and I wanted a quiet moment by myself to take it all in.

CHAPTER TWENTY-TWO

My first night in my new place! I explored the space, soaking in all the room I had compared to my condo in LA and appreciating Gertrude Miller's transformation of this second floor into an apartment, while preserving its original architectural design. I discovered how the moonlight came in through my bedroom transom window and the second bedroom's view through the branches of a tall oak tree down to the garden area.

I stepped out through the sunroom and onto the balcony. Moonlight sparkled on the water of the bay. Boats with running lights on returned to the marina. Lights from homes on Horseshoe Island sparkled in the distance, where families would be tucking little ones in for the night, tired from their day at the beach. The Rum

Runner would be bustling. And somewhere in that great, big, watery darkness was the *Black Pearl*. How far had Damien sailed since he left?

Turning to walk back into my living room, I paused. Trying to take in all the wonderful feelings. Home. My new home. I loved it already.

But ugh, now to unpack the rest of my things. That could wait until tomorrow afternoon. I'd be going to Paddy's Pub to help with Sunday brunch and then had no plans for the afternoon.

I made up my bed with fresh sheets and took a long hot shower instead of doing any more unpacking. But even after all that, I was still restless. I decided to check my emails.

Aubrey had shared her internet connection with me until I could get my own set up, and her password was on a note she left on the counter. How sweet of her. She'd also made note of a couple of the websites I'd expressed interest in, thinking I might search for Irish antiques for the pub. What started out as I'll just check my email and social media ended up with me searching one of those websites. I was drawn far down a rabbit hole in no time at all.

I heard Aubrey come in downstairs, and I texted her, asking if she could join me for a couple of minutes.

Within a few seconds, I heard her footsteps on the staircase and a knock at the landing door.

"Come on in. Door is open," I called out from where I sat on the couch with my laptop. "How was your walk?"

"Great. It's another gorgeous Florida night. I saw your lights on up here. I was expecting you to be fast asleep by now."

"So did I, but I started searching one of your websites for unique Irish pieces. And I've spent the last hour prowling around in the world of antique and artifact sites. Aubrey, you hinted that your great-aunt bought authentic antiques from dealers. Do you think she was just a savvy shopper, or could she have been duped? There are all sorts of disclaimers and warnings to beware of fraudulent sellers."

Aubrey nodded. "Let me run down and show you some things I've saved on my laptop. Be right back."

When Aubrey returned and opened her laptop, what she shared with me was eye-opening. There were dozens of current articles about the shadowy world of trafficking of cultural assets, antiquities, and artifacts. She took me to Interpol's website. Then to the US Immigration and Customs webpage, where updates on reintegration and restitution efforts were published. Databases full of items reported stolen or ownership disputed existed at the tips of my fingers. Photographs of pieces of historical or archaeological value that had gone missing from museums or government bodies appeared.

Aubrey leaned in and pointed at her screen. "You see, some of these were returned after being held by collectors whose heirs might not even know they were illegally obtained. Some have been exhibited in world-renowned museums for decades but were taken without authorization."

"This is crazy. I'm amazed it's all just right here," I said. "Look at this article about an art dealer and collector accused of running a huge antiquity trafficking network out of Southeast Asia."

"Now you can see why I check out this stuff, so I don't try to sell one of Aunt Gertrude's pieces on eBay, just like some of these articles point out has happened. If she got it, not knowing it wasn't meant to be taken out of the country, I know she'd want it returned to its rightful place."

"This is fascinating. And here, look…the Irish are fighting to have many treasures returned to them, too. But I think I'm safe buying certain antiques for the pub, like old historic architectural elements. And I came across some great old etchings, engravings, and prints that seem okay and the dealer is highly rated. What are your thoughts on these?" I spun my computer screen to show Aubrey what I'd looked at.

"Those seem fine." She Googled a new search term and up popped a new screen. "Now, if you see these, watch out!"

CHAPTER TWENTY-THREE

Since Fred usually showed up for the pub's Sunday Brunch, I texted him earlier this morning to please bring me a copy of the handwritten notes he'd gotten from Bernie's briefcase. In exchange, I promised to treat him and Fran to brunch.

When they arrived, he handed me a copy of the notes.

"You've given this information to Darnell?"

"I did," he said. "After our conversation on Friday, Barbara and I agreed with you that Darnell should see it. But I also kept a copy. But why do you need this?"

I hesitated to go into a lengthy conversation about where my thoughts took me, but I mentioned seeing some peculiar things at the plant and that I wanted to compare my own notes with Bernie's. Fred seemed satisfied with the reason and my reassurance that I would update him tomorrow if anything turned up.

I thanked him, saying, "This is all about helping figure out what happened on *Cruising Along* a week ago. I've discovered a few things that might have a connection to that mystery."

Now I needed Paddy's feedback on what I was thinking. Because my afternoon was going to be busy, I hoped he'd be able to go over it with me and then get it to Darnell. So, after the brunch rush was over, I took the copy of Bernie's handwritten notes Fred had given me up to Paddy's office.

From his office on the second floor at the back of the old bank building he'd turned into Paddy's Pub, I found Paddy standing at the windows that afforded him a breathtaking view down to the marina and the river. His desk was piled with paperwork and the day's receipts. I was grateful that now we'd have Aubrey's accounting skills to help give him more time to mingle with his guests and be the charming Irish host he was meant to be instead of being buried under never-ending paperwork.

Walking up to stand next to him, I said, "This view never gets old."

"You've got that right," he murmured. "I'm a lucky bloke. Now, what are you still doin' here? I thought you were going over to see Sophia and Jack."

"I'm going there as soon as I show you this paper and explain a couple of things because I'd like you to give this to Darnell today with my comments on it."

Paddy sat down at his desk to scan the paper. As I explained, Barbara had found it in Bernie's possessions and it appeared to be issues with some irregularities he noted with the casket plants operations.

"She said his concerns with things there were weighing heavily on him and that he had plans to stay in Seaside Cove and visit the plant after the weekend."

As we went over the paper, I added a few comments of my own to help Paddy understand where my thoughts were leading me. "See this remark about increasing costs of material expenses and his thought of reaching out to different suppliers and negotiating new contracts? That's an accounting item that I'm not really that concerned with. But this specific appointment with Terry to discuss the random additions to the trucking company's billings over the past year is. And his question about increasing mistakes in bills of lading fits in with something I stumbled into at a little diner in Woodville."

I scribbled a quick note on the paper to let Darnell know I was hoping to get further information for him.

"Busy lass you've been," Paddy said, leaning back his chair. "But why were you at a diner way over by Woodville?"

"Eve was going to the Woodville Casket Company for research on her next book, so I tagged along," I said. "And we had lunch afterward."

"You went to the casket company? Why on earth did you do that?" Paddy asked.

"The opportunity presented itself. I'll explain later but let me finish this for now."

I sensed Paddy was skeptical that any of this had something to do with Bernie's death, but I plowed ahead, being sure to point out the starred comment that Bernie had made to speak with Earleen about the disgruntled employee concerns she'd shared with him. I penciled in the fact that I'd met her when we visited the plant.

"Why is this your concern, Katie?"

"I was doing some online research last night, and I'm thinking there might be some dots to connect."

"Sure, and it's possible that having these notes on what Bernie was concerned about at the plant could, in some convoluted way, lead to why someone killed him, but I'm not keen on you involving yourself so closely.

Let Darnell figure out how things might connect," Paddy said.

"I will let him, but this afternoon, I think I may be able to get some further clues that will help him even more. And it's perfectly safe, Uncle Paddy. Don't worry. See you later."

CHAPTER TWENTY-FOUR

I'd arranged to meet Sophia at their boat in the marina, and when I got there, Jack was hosing down the deck.

"Hey Katie, how's it going? Come on board," Jack called out.

"Jack, can you tell me anything about what you told Darnell this weekend?" My question came out more bluntly than I intended. But if today was to go the way I hoped I really needed to find out more.

"Sorry, Katie. Much as I'd like to, I really shouldn't because you're not in law enforcement," Jack said. "Why are you asking?"

"I don't know for sure if what I've discovered has anything to do with Bernie's death, but I think it might." I proceeded to tell him what I'd pulled together, including what I had been researching last night.

Jack's expression grew serious, and he leaned in closer as he absorbed my words. He asked me to promise that I would not repeat what he was about to divulge. "When I got back to my office earlier this week, I learned that an undercover FBI agent had been in Seaside Cove since the Wednesday before the festival. He was tracking Damien Falcon and the woman he had with him on the *Black Pearl*. The agent asked for Chief Darnell's help stalling him as long as he could. But since Darnell had no legitimate reason to detain him or his craft, he was free to sail away."

"Why were they being followed?" I asked.

"For trafficking in just the type of objects you were researching last night. We're working with several governmental agencies because these types of investigations get very complicated."

"Oh, my gosh! So, that confirms one suspicion I had. But why weren't they just arrested?"

"Remember, this is an ongoing investigation. They are just one possible link in this shadowy world, and in an ideal world, they will lead the authorities to more criminals, he said. "There are many situations where we spend years building a case only to have it fall apart, too. So don't say a word about this, and don't do anything to jeopardize our investigation."

Now I knew I had to go ahead with my plan.

CHAPTER TWENTY-FIVE

Luckily, I had the lipstick Victoria left at the pub Friday night to use as an excuse to get on the Ingalls' boat. But I wanted a partner in crime, and Sophia eagerly agreed to accompany me when she heard what I hoped to achieve. Her being with me added a protective layer of plausibility.

"Oh, you didn't have to bother," Victoria said when she saw I was returning her lipstick. "I probably owe you an apology for my behavior on Friday night. I was a little tipsy. I hadn't eaten much all week, what with losing my ex-husband in such a tragic event. Then finding out the company I now owned was worth much less than I expected. My husband has been on my case to keep it. But forgive me. I blather on."

"Have you decided to stay and straighten things out

at Woodville? Or will you and Richard be leaving again soon?" I asked.

"We're planning on leaving tomorrow, but only for a short cruise. Against my better judgment, but at the urging of my husband, I'm going to let Bernie's cousin Terry continue managing the place for a few days. I've wanted to get out of that business for a long time. I hope to find a good commercial broker when we return and see what I should do to get the best price. Richard is all for keeping it and spending the next year or two revamping it. Maybe expand into offering funeral vaults and urns for ashes…ugh! I just want to be done with it!"

"You know, that's not a bad idea. You have the distribution channels to the funeral homes. You might benefit by adding a product they use more frequently now." My eyes took in the disorder here on the boat's outside deck. There were cushions askew, used glassware and plates out, and beach towels in a pile.

Victoria held her palm up. "I know, Katie. I'm just so overwhelmed at this point that I can't think straight. Richard has been putting up with my angst this week, so I've agreed to let him whisk me away for a few days."

"How nice that must be," Sophia said in a dreamy voice. "When Jack and I retire, we'd like to do more traveling on our boat, too. Or maybe get a bigger one like yours. But then you need a crew to help and all that, right?"

"We make do without anyone else most times," Victoria said as she rearranged the dirty dishes and kicked the towels into a smaller pile. "Richard is a skilled mechanic and boater, so he can handle many things by himself. But for the longer trips, we hire someone. I hope you get to enjoy the boating life as much as I have."

"Where have you all traveled?" Sophia pushed the thing we were here to learn. "I've been keeping a log for posterity, but right now, it's only filled with ports here on the panhandle. We hope to head to St. Pete and then maybe Naples soon."

Victoria's demeanor brightened. "We keep a log. Time flies by, and it's so fun to remember where we've been and who visited us. Would you and Katie sign our guest log? And you can take a peek at the ports we've been to. Richard's gong-ho about seeing more exotic ones, and I'm most definitely up for it."

"Your friend Damien is on his way to Peru, I believe. Or was it Ecuador?" I asked hoping to catch her in giving us more information.

Victoria hesitated. "Hmm…you know, I'm not sure. He's always traveling. We've run into him in quite a few other ports, believe it or not. Now, that man really does it in style. When I get my money out of the coffin busi-ness, I have some destinations in mind."

"Small world," I said. "Like, where did you run into him?"

"The Caymans. St. Lucia. Aruba."

"Wow! Places I can only hope to visit someday," Sophia said.

"We'd better get out of your hair, Victoria. What's Richard up to today?" I asked.

"He took Terry out golfing. He felt bad for how I treated him at the plant these past few days. It's just, oh, I don't know, I have a weird feeling about the guy. But Richard wanted to assure him that he was still going to have a job and that I would be out of his hair for a few days."

"And where's that log for us to sign? You said inside?" Sophia asked.

"Oh yes, to your left, on the small desk." Victoria's mood shifted again, and she turned her back to us to plump up the deck cushions.

Later, looking over the photos I snapped of the Ingalls' port and visitor logbook, I knew they would give Jack's associate concrete information. I didn't send the photos to Jack just yet though. Learning that Victoria and Richard planned on leaving tomorrow prompted me to make a phone call to Aubrey to get Josh and Sean's cell phone numbers.

CHAPTER TWENTY-SIX

An early Monday morning text arrived with a cell phone number on it. Sean came through! I had needed his help in trying to reach the truck driver Eve, Greg, and I met at the Woodville diner. I hoped Sean could find some shipping paperwork with information on how I could find him, and he came through. I called Roy. He remembered me but said he was on the road and would look up the information I requested when he had a chance to pull over.

Within an hour, I received an address, and when I Googled it, it proved to be just what I expected. It was time to take this to Darnell myself. Hopefully, he had already gotten a chance to consider my comments on Bernie's notes.

"I'm sure these points of Bernie's were concerning

items for him," Darnell said as soon as I closed his office door and sat down. "And I appreciate you adding some context to them for me to consider. But I've got the information and now I think it best that Fred also take this directly to Victoria since she is the owner. That would seem to make the most sense."

"I respectfully disagree because of not only what Barbara and Fred told me about the situation on Friday night but also because of what I've put together since then. If my theory doesn't check out, then by all means, take them to Victoria, but please give me a few minutes more to lay out what I've come across. Remember your motto of the power of the public. Well, I'm the public and I have some information I think you need to hear."

Darnell laughed before resting his clasped hands on his desk. "I'm all ears."

My heart raced as I dumped the weight of this information on Darnell. I understood the importance of presenting it all in a cohesive and logical manner. As I started recounting the events that had led me here, I made sure to arrange them in a timeline that would make sense to him and fill in any gaps in his knowledge. Every detail had to be accounted for. But as I delved into a narration of the clues and hints of possibilities, it became overwhelming. I struggled to keep my words coherent and organized. I wanted to make sure I didn't start straying off on unnecessary tangents.

I must have given him enough convincing evidence because his first words were, "I'm impressed, Katie. Here, I thought all this wasn't connected. There was Mr. Falcon sailing away in his *Black Pearl* and the FBI tracking his moves in one hand…and Bernard Green's death on the other. Which, I'll confess, I still strongly considered to be a tragic accident until you brought me all of this. You've laid out an impressive case for them being connected."

After I mentioned that I had a plan that might work to stall the Ingalls' departure today, Darnell gave me a warning look. "Dare I ask what you did to accomplish that, or would I rather not know?"

"Let's just say it might not work. But if it does…ignorance is bliss."

"Don't give me that, Katie Murphy. With what you've told me, you could be in danger yourself."

After leaving the police station, I didn't know what to do with myself. It was out of my hands for now. I puttered around the apartment, continuing to feather my nest. Aubrey was downstairs working, so I didn't want to bother her.

Later that afternoon, I decided to take my golf cart through the marina. I hoped Josh had figured out something to make Richard think he needed a repair on his boat. My hope was he'd find some little thing wrong on their boat that might delay their departure by at least a day. It wasn't looking good, though, because I saw that Victoria was helping Richard prepare their vessel to leave its mooring spot.

"Hey Katie, come to say goodbye? It was nice to see you and Sophia yesterday. I may see you in a few days," Victoria said.

Richard appeared on the back deck and greeted me as well. "Not if I can whisk my love away from all the worry she's been going through here. Let's just say we'll see you when we see you!"

I wished them safe travels, but inside, I was disappointed. It was a lot to ask of Josh to make up something on their boat that needed immediate attention and would take at least a day…but I had tried. Now I crossed my fingers that things going on behind the scenes were moving swiftly.

And they were because a call came in from Darnell letting me know he was on his way back from Woodville and wanted to give me a brief summary of what had transpired in the last couple of hours. He'd emailed Jack my photographs I'd taken of the travel log pages from the Ingalls' boat. Jack had promptly forwarded it to the agent working on Damian and Ariana's case, along with a detailed explanation. Darnell had also made sure Jack had the location of the Savannah warehouse that the truck driver had given me. The FBI raided the warehouse and found artifacts hidden in Woodville Caskets, along with paperwork directing them to be repackaged and delivered to a residence on Hilton Head Island.

Darnell convinced the Woodville Police to go with him to the factory and question Terry Green. "Katie, the guy was on such a razor-thin edge, and we approached him at just the right time. You'll be glad to know that he broke down and confessed to his part in the smuggling operations. He is currently in Woodville police custody and singing like a lark. I see him being offered a plea deal to testify against his partner in crime in the very near future."

"Chief, you move fast! I'm breathless. I couldn't have imagined it would all fall into place like this. That Terry Green crumbled so easily is the icing on the cake. How did that go down?" I asked.

Darnell said he'd fill in details later today, but right

now, he was in a hurry because he had a County Sheriff's Marine Unit waiting for him.

It was late Monday night before Darnell let me know he was off duty and on his way to join me at Paddy's Pub. Uncle Paddy was on bartender duty tonight, but since the place was set to close in less than an hour and there were only three customers left, he took a seat on a stool next to me to enjoy a pint while we waited.

I suggested Darnell come here because I wanted Paddy to hear everything. I took the time to catch him up on how Sophia and I had gotten a peek into the recent ports that the Ingalls had been at. Then, I explained how they might overlap with places Damien had been.

"But how would you know where Damien traveled, and why would it matter?" Paddy asked.

"I don't know where the *Black Pearl* has been, but I have good reason to believe it matters now. I just wanted to get enough proof to make Darnell take my idea seriously," I said. "I'll let the chief tell you more about why that might matter when he gets here."

"Ah, sure, you're alright for now, Katie. But what

would me family back in Ireland do if you came here to help me in my golden years and ended up mixed up in murder cases and get yourself hurt? I was dead serious on Sunday when I asked you to let Darnell handle things. Don't want you puttin' yourself in any danger, lass. I've seen how scoundrels operate, and it ain't pretty."

"Uncle Paddy, that's so sweet, but I'm fine!" I reached to kiss him on his rosy cheek. "I love you for worrying about me."

Darnell came strolling in and called out. "Hey, barkeep. I'm one thirsty man. Figure you can get off your butt and pour me one?"

Paddy hopped off his stool and gave a crisp salute. "Aye, sir, it'll be up in a jiffy. The usual, is it?"

Once Darnell had settled in next to me, he quizzed us. "I'll give you three choices to guess who I arrested today. Victoria, Richard, or both of them?"

"Arrested?" Paddy practically shouted. "For Bernie's murder?"

I was almost bouncing in my seat. The whole case was breaking wide open at last, and I was ecstatic to know an arrest had been made. "Paddy, the chief got a boat ride this afternoon. The Sheriff's Marine Unit helped him chase down the Ingalls' boat."

"By the saints," Paddy exclaimed. "What next? Come on, you two, spill the story while I fetch us another pint. I want to hear every last bit of it."

"I'll bet it was Richard," I said. "Paddy, who do you think murdered Bernard Green?"

"I'll choose Bernie's old wife," Paddy answered as he poured our beers. "Isn't that often the way of it?"

"You win, Katie. It was Richard," Darnell said. "And you were proved right about what you noted during your casket factory visit. That whole thing really was the link between what I thought were two separate cases."

"So that Damien fella was involved in the murder too?" Paddy asked.

"Not in the murder. At least not directly." A crooked grin slowly appeared on Darnell's face. "But I'm sure he'll be angry when he finds out what his buddy Richard did to keep his fingers in the money pot. I knew about the FBI's investigation into Damien Falcon and that Jack let me know there had been an undercover agent trailing him, but I couldn't share that information with either of you earlier. It was too risky for the agent if it got out. Plus, Homeland Security was in on this all, and I didn't want to mess up their work either. But hold on, I'm jumping around too much."

Paddy bid farewell to the final patrons with a warm smile, while Darnell took a slow, satisfying sip of his beer. I followed suit, indulging in the crisp, refreshing taste. It had been a long couple of days, but now I felt grateful that everything had fallen perfectly into place.

"Funny how white-framed sunglasses catch the eye," Darnell began.

"So, you saw those too?" I remembered them because it was notably uncommon among boaters.

"I did, and so did Josh. He couldn't identify any of the men talking with the captain about the mechanical issues on Friday because their backs were to him. But he noted one of them had white framed sunglasses perched on top of his head. Like I always say…no detail is too small."

Darnell went on to explain that the sunglass detail pointed the finger at Richard because he was then aware of the faulty compressor on Bernie's boat. And that his devious mind formulated a plan to use the work being done as a cover for murdering Bernie through carbon monoxide poisoning."

Paddy's perplexed expression was almost laughable so Darnell explained why Richard would want to poison Bernie. "He was getting close to finding out about the illegalities going on at the Woodville plant. If Bernie was out of the picture, Richard knew Victoria would be in charge of the place, and he could manipulate her."

"Richard must have snuck onboard *Cruising Along*

while Bernie and Barbara were still at the dance Saturday night," I said eager to put more pieces into place. "I knew he walked Victoria home early because she didn't feel well. And she told me he was good with mechanical things on boats, so it would have been simple to mess with the compressor and take the batteries out of the detectors while Bernie and Barbara were having a great time dancing."

But Paddy was still confused. "Why did Richard want his wife to run a casket company when she just wanted to sell it?"

Darnell explained that Richard, knowing the Green family story about smuggling booze into the country in caskets during the prohibition, suggested his acquaintance, Damien Falcon, do the same with the artifacts and valuable pieces of art he was stealing or trading for around the world.

Paddy slowly nodded, showing he was getting the bigger picture now.

"How he knew Damien was a smuggler, I'm not sure, but I'll get help from the feds to figure that piece out," Darnell said. "Richard knew that his wife's ownership of the plant would allow him to access the place anytime. And he knew cousin Terry would be more than willing to help. He was bitter and disgruntled about always being treated like a second-class member of the Green family."

"That's why he didn't want to sell the place like Victoria was ready to do," I added. "It would be an end to his gig, and he'd be cut off from the extra money it was bringing him. Was she shocked when you boarded their boat?"

"She sure was," Darnell said. "Imagine being in her spot. I kept a close eye on her reaction, and it seemed real, but to be honest, I'm not ruling out her being a part of it at this point."

"Do you think Richard considered taking her out of the picture? Like an overboard accident while they were at sea?" Paddy asked. "If he was working on her to keep the factory and had killed Bernie to do that, where would he stop? Get rid of her, and he'd inherit the whole thing."

"Yikes, Uncle Paddy, your mind is going in a whole other direction. But what a perfect solution that would have been for him. No more arguing in women's bathrooms."

Paddy and Darnell both looked at me in total confusion.

"Just another dot I connected," I said. It was getting more complicated, and right now, they didn't need to know about the argument I'd overheard between Richard and Victoria.

"I'll be busy the next few days," Darnell said. "I'm in contact with the truck driver, Roy. He and Earleen are going to help find other suspicious shipments. The trail might allow the authorities to find more stolen property and return it."

"So, was it the sword from Damien's boat that the feds found in the Savannah warehouse?" I asked.

"Yes, along with a Columbian pottery piece. Jack told me the FBI would be trailing Damien and Ariana through the Panama Canal, figuring he was heading to South America for more artifacts. If they think Damian gets wind of the fact that Richard and his link to the smuggling operation have been exposed, they'll board his yacht either prior to it entering the Panama Canal or on the other side. With the Savannah warehouse evidence and the trail of transport you put together, they have enough to get a warrant now, but catching him with illegal goods on board would be best."

I was relieved and had a clear conscience when I learned this information. If I had wrongly accused innocent people, I would have regretted it. Things clicked when I saw the neighbor kids playing hide and seek. They were hiding in plain sight, just like the missing artifact from the

Black Pearl that caught my attention once, then was missing on parade day when I went to use the powder room. A small detail but a big one. And I had to laugh when I considered that another bathroom visit helped solve a murder!

"Can you tell me more about your interaction with Terry Green?" I asked.

"With another beer I will," Darnell teased.

After Darnell was served, he told us Terry felt threatened by Richard. The operation had been going on for well over a year and he'd actively participated by driving to other drop-off ports like Pensacola or Mobile to pick up loot from Richard. Terry explained that times were different when both owners were off living their lives. But with Bernie gone and the company going to Victoria, her nosing around to see what was going on unnerved him.

"And I can see that Richard didn't want to sell so he could keep up the smuggling," Paddy said.

"That's right. Terry told me that Richard took him golfing and said he was taking Victoria out of the area for a few days to let things cool down. But when I explained the evidence we already had and that it meant jail time for him, Terry figured he had more to gain by cooperating."

"Well then, things seemed to come together, except

for the arrest of Mr. Falcon," Paddy said. "Good job, you two. Another one for you, Katie?"

Darnell was wound up and wanted to talk more, but I was ready to leave. Paddy locked the pub's door behind me. I left them to their police talk, glad that I could rest knowing things were now in the right hands.

CHAPTER TWENTY-SEVEN

Aubrey and Blaire asked me to join them on their Wednesday evening walk, but I had to decline because Uncle Paddy and Aunt Maeve were coming over to see my new place.

It was nice to be in this part of town. The people-watching was great, whether they were on the sidewalk in front of the house, enjoying the park, or strolling on the walking trail along the river. With my new binoculars, I spent time scanning the boats in the bay and the fishing activity on the pier.

Earlier today I'd hit up the Farmers Market on the green space at our municipal center. I fought the temptation to drop in on Chief Darnell's office while I was there to find out if Damien and Ariana had been arrested yet. I'd not spoken to him since his Monday night information dump at Paddy's Pub.

Barbara gave me a call this morning to thank me for all the support I showed her during this difficult period. I suggested we grab coffee, but she couldn't because she and Fred were heading to the Keys. Fred wanted to put his brother's home on the market as soon as possible.

"What is he doing with the *Cruising Along?*" I asked.

"He's dealing with a boat broker in the Keys because it will sell faster there. Bernie's captain is taking the boat down."

"Hey, you know…in all the busyness of the past few days, I forgot about the captain. What happened to him?"

"To be honest, Katie, in my eyes, he was the main suspect," she said. "But Darnell cleared him after Richard was apprehended. He left for Destin on Saturday night to visit with family, expecting to return and take us home to the Keys. But that all changed overnight. The poor man was afraid to show his face in Seaside. Afraid he'd get arrested."

"Well, Barbara, I wish you the best. And you got my interest peaked with that tarot thing. Maybe I'll learn more about it one day. What changed when you talked to Ella a week ago?"

"Me." A soft giggle came through the phone line. "My

attitude and perspective. Even an old broad like me can change."

I first caught sight of Maeve and Paddy out in front of the house. She was showing Paddy the flower beds, bending to smell the blooms. Then she pointed down the street to Eve's home. Paddy nodded and smiled, jostling the large, gift-wrapped package he carried in his arms.

"Going to come in and enjoy the view from up here?" I called down to them. "Stairs are around the back side."

"Ah, Katie, tis a lovely spot for you. We're so happy you've found a place," Maeve said when she arrived at my front hall.

I gave them a quick tour of the place. My own touches were making it feel more like my own every day. We were in the bedroom when Paddy handed me the gift he'd been carrying.

Maeve said, "This is what I've been working on since you moved to Seaside Cove. I know how much you loved the quilt on my guest bed, and it was a blessing to make this one for you to use in your new home."

My heart grew full, and my eyes teared up as I unwrapped the package. Inside was a quilt made in the lovely pattern and colors of the one I'd slept under in the guest room at Kenmare Cottage. I hugged it tight against my chest and breathed in the smell of love woven in every stitch.

"This is a perfect housewarming gift," I said. "I can't thank you enough, and I will always treasure it."

"Then come here and give me a big hug, my Katie girl."

A knock at my door startled us out of what had turned into a group hug, with Uncle Paddy awkwardly joining in and my new quilt getting squished in the process.

Winnie stood there with a big bouquet of flowers. "These here are fresh-picked, and I figured they'd look the best in your new place. Why, look who's here! I didn't see your golf cart in front."

"No, we walked over. It's such a lovely evening, and the exercise does us good."

"I reckon I should have walked too, but I'm plum tuckered out. Spent all day wrangling the animals at the shelter, and they wore me down. Lord knows I could stand to lose a few pounds. Why this is a right nice place. Except for all them dang stairs. But hey, you're young." Winnie plopped down on my sofa.

I set out drinks and appetizers for all of us. I'm not much for cooking or baking but I can arrange easy appetizers and now that charcuterie boards are all on trend, I'm good with that.

As Winnie reached across for an olive Maeve said, "What are those scratches on your arm?"

"Darn black kitten got wild with me. Cute little rascal but feisty as all get out. And bad luck, too. Black as a raven. Hope someone adopts her before Halloween. Don't want her bringing any bad luck round the shelter. Hey Katie, maybe you could use a little buddy up here in this fancy house."

"Thank you for the flowers. They are gorgeous. And no thank you on the pet idea."

Winnie chuckled. "I get you Katie. But speakin' of Halloween, have you heard if they got that mess cleared up about who owns the old McCracken place?"

"That's near here, isn't it?" I asked.

"Yep, and there was talk of using it for a Halloween haunted house tour," Winnie said.

"I haven't heard anything about ownership," Maeve said. "But what a beauty it must have been. It has such good bones. So sad to see it fall apart. And that yard, dear me! Weeds, wild grass, overgrown shrubs. Just disgusts me," Maeve said.

"That's the family that built the bank where the pub is now, right?" Paddy asked.

"Yep, and the old lady's ghost still haunts the bank." Winnie cackled with a smirk on her face as she gleefully rubbed her hands together. "Oh, but that house could be the best darn place to have a good Halloween scare set up. Even for adults. I could play the creepy old bitty."

"I'll just bet you could!" Maeve said. "Who's looking into the issue?"

"Good question. Reckon' it would be the parks department. Hmm…or not. Maybe the local high school theater group? They try to put on things like that."

Our conversation lasted until the sky was painted in shades of orange as the sun began to set over the bay.

As the summer days passed, Main Street transformed into a sea of red, white, and blue in anticipation of the Fourth of July. American flags fluttered proudly on every street corner while bunting adorned the buildings. The entire street was transformed into a patriotic wonderland.

The retailers had gone all out with their window displays. Quilts featuring intricate star blocks in bold red, white, and blue hues were proudly displayed in Marge's Sew-Sew shop. The souvenir store stocked up on stars and stripes visors, Fourth-of-July-themed T-shirts, and endless picnic and party products for the tourists, including the iconic red Solo cups. Books in all sorts of genres, but with fireworks and flags on their covers, filled the bookstore's display. As I walked down Main Street, I couldn't help but feel a sense of excitement about the upcoming celebration.

I was proud of our mannequin, Mel, who'd been transformed into Uncle Sam with a top hat, tailcoat, and striped trousers. Again, he tempted locals and tourists to take photographs with him. He'd proven his worth in marketing value and was always good for lots of clicks and exposure on social media.

The celebration of America's independence went off with a bang, so to speak. The fireworks were top-notch, but it was the grand finale that stole the show. A spectacle of lights and colors burst in the night sky, casting a warm glow over the faces of hundreds of those gathered on the grassy slope below my little balcony.

Weeks more passed before newspaper and online articles about the arrest of Damien Falcon and Ariana Lozano on the western coast of South America began to appear. South American artifacts that had been stolen over two years ago from the Colombian National Museum in Bogotá were among the evidence found onboard the *Black Pearl*.

When the capture was finally made public, Jack was free to divulge the details to us. He revealed that Damien had been kept completely unaware of what had befallen his partner-in-crime, Richard Ingalls, thanks to some carefully orchestrated tactics implemented by the FBI. Even Victoria had played a role in covering up the truth to allow agents to not only charge Damian and Ariana but to uncover a crime ring operating in Bogota.

"The artifacts were stored by the Columbian criminals and hidden in the country until the heat was off. Then they would use smugglers like Damien to get the stolen goods out of the country," Jack explained.

"Didn't Richard make any attempt to warn Damien about being watched?" I asked Jack as we shared a booth with Paddy and Darnell at Paddy's Pub.

"I highly doubt he had any opportunity to do that once he was picked up. He was very closely guarded, and Victoria was on our side in this. She was beside herself when she found out what her husband had been doing. Sure, Damien knew about Bernard Green's murder, but he had no idea that Richard was the one charged with it. So, he had no reason to expect contact from Richard during this time."

I learned that Victoria had found a buyer for the Woodville Casket Company and had gone back to live in Miami. I felt bad for Fred Green. He lost his brother and, with him, the ties to his family's business. But time marches on.

And so it did for all of us. Tyler taught me how to

handle my own jet ski, and Jesse helped me convince Ella Winchester to consider putting several of her art pieces for sale in the Coffee Corner. Maddie and Sean's wedding celebration went off without a hitch. They married in the gazebo in Seaside Cove Park and celebrated with dinner and dancing in the banquet rooms at Paddy's Pub. Fall arrived, and the yellow school buses started roaming the streets again. Our book club met monthly. Winnie kept up her volunteering. Jack and Sophia didn't find a second home here yet but were still looking.

Efforts for the McCracken house, with its peeling paint and spooky aura, to be used as a Halloween haunted house were well underway. Surprisingly, Aubrey was spearheading the effort and had enlisted the help of her next-door neighbor, an attorney, to navigate the legal complexities surrounding ownership of the house. In gratitude for her assistance, Aubrey offered to babysit her neighbor's children, often persuading me to join her in watching over them.

My life here was full and happy. And despite being thousands of miles away from my family in Ireland, I kept in touch through video chats. However, my attempts were often thwarted by my mischievous green-eyed buddy who invariably decided to saunter across my laptop in front of the screen, demanding attention and interrupting conversations during these family visits.

As I lounged on my couch, the glow of the television casting a warm light on Raven's sleek black coat, my mind drifted back to that memorable evening in June when Maeve and Paddy came to see my new apartment.

Winnie had shown up too, with a bouquet of fresh-cut flowers from her garden and with scratched-up arms from a feisty black kitten at the animal shelter. Well, one thing led to another and with a little persuasion from Maeve and Paddy and assurances from Aubrey that a cute furry kitten would be welcomed to roam both floors of the house, I adopted Raven. Now, as she lies curled up in my lap, I know it was one of the best decisions I had ever made.

She will make the cutest Halloween companion in fall when we celebrate Raising Spirits!

NEXT IN KATIE MURPHY
COZY MYSTERY SERIES!

A KATIE MURPHY COZY MYSTERY
RAISING SPIRITS
IRISh PUB
SUZANNE BOLDEN

Check it out!

ABOUT THE AUTHOR

Here are a few ways to reach me…I'd love to stay connected!

Please <u>sign up for my monthly newsletter</u>. I'll share things about my life…both personal as Brenda Felber and professionally as my pen name Suzanne Bolden.
Like/follow Suzanne on her Facebook page

If you follow me on these two, you'll be automatically notified when new releases are available.
Bookbub
<u>Amazon Author Central</u>

Check out my website <u>www.suzannebolden.com</u>

Thank you for reading my books. If you enjoyed them, a review is much appreciated!

ALSO BY SUZANNE BOLDEN

Katie Murphy Cozy Mystery Series

#1 Pour Decisions

#2 Pick Yar Poison

#3 Raising Spirits

#4 Auld Lang Stein

#5 A Wee Lepre-Con

#6 Paws for a Pint

7 The Elf Did It

#8 Matrimony and Malice

#9 Read Between the Lines